FRANK BARRETT

Frank Barrett is the Travel Editor of
The Mail on Sunday and has worked as a writer and
journalist for many years. He has won five major
Travel Writer of the Year awards and has written
numerous travel books and holiday guides.
Frank makes regular appearances on television and
radio, presenting and commenting on travel issues.

His great interest in children's literature inspired him
to combine his love of travelling with children's books
to create *Where Was Wonderland?*

D0273755

To Sheila, Dan and Jessica - *'Dulce Domum'*.

First published in Great Britain in 1997 by Hamlyn Children's Books
an imprint of Reed International Books Limited
Michelin House, 81 Fulham Road, London SW3 6RB
and Auckland and Melbourne.

Text © 1997 Frank Barrett
Map illustrations © 1997 John Woodcock

ISBN 0 6005 9345 2

A CIP catalogue record is available for this title from the British Library.

Printed and bound in Great Britain by Cox and Wyman Ltd, Reading, Berks.

Where was Wonderland?

A TRAVELLER'S GUIDE TO THE SETTINGS
of CLASSIC CHILDREN'S BOOKS

FRANK BARRETT

HAMLYN

ACKNOWLEDGEMENTS

The author and publisher have taken all possible care to trace the copyright holders of all material used in this book, and to make acknowledgement of their use. We apologise for any omissions which may have occurred; they will be corrected in subsequent editions, provided notification is sent to the publisher.

For permission to reproduce text quotations in this book, acknowledgement is due to the following:

Rex Collings Publishers and David Higham Associates for quotations from *Watership Down* by Richard Adams on pages 21, 22 and 23; William Heinemann for quotations from the books *Thomas and Gordon* and *Thomas and the Breakdown Train* by The Reverend W. Awdry on pages 29, 30 and 31 © W H Books Ltd; Great Ormond Street Hospital for quotations from *Peter Pan* by J M Barrie on pages 37; David Higham Associates and Jonathan Cape Publishers Ltd for quotations from *Danny, Champion of the World* by Roald Dahl, text © Felicity Dahl and the other executors of the Estate of Roald Dahl 1975 on pages 59, 60 and 61; Frederick Warne & Co for quotations from *The Tale of Samuel Whiskers, The Tale of Mrs Tiggy-winkle* and *The Tale of Jemima Puddle-duck* by Beatrix Potter on pages 67 and 68; Curtis Brown Group Ltd for quotations from *Carrie's War* on pages 76 and 77. Reproduced by permission of Curtis Brown Group Ltd, London, on behalf of Nina Bawden. Copyright © Nina Bawden 1973; quotations from *The Wind in the Willows* on pages 85 and 86, by Kenneth Grahame © The University Chest, Oxford, by permission of Curtis Brown Group Ltd, London; Victor Gollancz Ltd for quotations from *The Sheep-Pig* by Dick King-Smith on pages 104 and 105; HarperCollins Publishers Ltd for quotations from *The Lion, the Witch and the Wardrobe* by C. S. Lewis on pages 119 and 121; Methuen Children's Books for quotations from *Winnie-the-Pooh* by A A Milne on pages 134 and 135; Chatto & Windus Publishers Ltd for quotations from *Cider with Rosie* by Laurie Lee on pages 152 and 153; Film Rights Ltd in association with Laurence Fitch Ltd for quotations from *The Hundred and One Dalmatians* on pages 159 and 161; Jonathan Cape Publishers Ltd and the Arthur Ransome Estate for quotations from *Swallows and Amazons* by Arthur Ransome on pages 168 and 169; excerpts from *The Little Prince* by Antoine de Saint-Exupéry on pages 184, 185 and 186, copyright 1943 and renewed 1971 by Harcourt Brace and Company, reprinted by permission of the publisher, also William Heinemann Ltd for the same quotations from *The Little Prince*.

For permission to reproduce artwork in this book, acknowledgements are due to the following:

Front cover illustration by Arthur Rackham from *Alice's Adventures in Wonderland* is reproduced with kind permission of his family; William Heinemann Ltd for the illustration of *Thomas the Tank Engine* by John Kenney © W H Books Ltd on page 28; Jonathan Cape Publishers Ltd for the illustration by Quentin Blake from *Danny, The Champion of the World* © Quentin Blake 1994 on page 59; Curtis Brown Group Ltd for permission to reproduce illustrations by E H Shepard from *The Wind in the Willows*, copyright under the Berne Convention, on pages 84 and 87. Illustrations by E H Shepard from *The Wind in the Willows* by Kenneth Grahame reprinted with the permission of Atheneum Books for Young Readers, an imprint of Simon & Schuster Children's Publishing Division. Copyright 1933 Charles Scribner's Sons, copyright renewed © 1961 Ernest H Shepard. Illustrations by E H Shepard from *Winnie-the-Pooh*, copyright under the Berne Convention, reproduced by permission of Curtis Brown, London on page 135 and 137. Illustrations by E H Shepard from *Winnie-the-Pooh* by A A Milne, copyright 1926 by E P Dutton, renewed 1954 by A A Milne. Used by permission of Dutton Children's Books, a division of Penguin Books USA Inc. Also to Cecilie Dressler Verlag and Livraria Martin Fontes Editora Ltda for permission to reproduce in Germany and Brazil respectively; Frederick Warne & Co. for permission to reproduce the illustration from *The Tale of Mrs Tiggy-winkle* by Beatrix Potter on page 67, copyright © F. Warne & Co., 1905. Beatrix Potter; Film Rights Ltd in association with Laurence Fitch Ltd for permission to reproduce the illustration from *The Hundred and One Dalmatians* by Anne Grahame-Johnstone on page 160; William Heinemann Ltd for permission to reproduce illustrations from *The Little Prince* by Antoine de Saint-Exupéry on pages 183 and 186. Illustrations from *The Little Prince* by Antoine de Saint-Exupéry copyright 1943 and renewed 1971 by Harcourt Brace and Company, reprinted by permission of the publisher.

CONTENTS

FOREWORD

P eter Pan told Wendy that to find the Neverland she should take the 'second to the right, and straight on till morning' – not very precise directions. As J M Barrie noted, '. . . even birds, carrying maps and consulting them at windy corners could not have found it with these instructions.' But while you may never find the Neverland, you may be as surprised as I was to discover that the home of the Darling family is just a short walk from a London tube station. And the house still looks today much as it would have done almost 100 years ago, when Wendy, John and Michael flew with Peter out of the upstairs nursery window into the night.

This discovery made me wonder how many other children's books had real-life locations. Could I, for example, find Alice's Wonderland? Indeed I could – the entrance to the rabbit hole which led to the Queen of Hearts and the Mad Hatter's tea party lies in a field just off the Oxford ring road. Curiouser and curiouser, as Alice might have said.

Other favourite books of my childhood quickly turned out to have genuine locations. The first 'proper book' I can remember reading was *The Hundred And One Dalmatians* by Dodie Smith. My mother and father gave it me as a Christmas present when I was eight and almost at once I fell completely in love with it. It was a book I went back to again and again, allowing the story to carry me off to that dreamy 'other world' for which good books are the only passport. I recently searched the book out, and just holding it once more in my hands rekindled all those old fond memories.

Its setting seemed to me then as fantastic as its story of 101 dogs. As far as I was concerned, Regent's Park might have been on the other side of the moon. Had someone, all those years ago, actually taken me there and pointed to a handsome white terraced house (just like the one pictured in the original edition of the book) and said 'There, that is the home of Mr and Mrs Dearly and their dalmatians!', I might well have fainted away with pleasure and excitement. When, last year, I did exactly this, the magic quickly returned. With immense pleasure I wandered up and down the pavement outside, wide-eyed: eight years old all over again.

I have become accustomed to this feeling while writing this book. Whether it's been discovering Eeyore's Gloomy Place, locating Toad Hall, or exploring the real Secret Garden, visiting the places connected with favourite childhood stories has been a truly extraordinary experience. My two children have accompanied me on these literary safaris and they found the discoveries – and the occasional piece of detective work that was necessary – just as delightful as I did. Inspired by each location, we inevitably returned to the book and read it again with renewed enjoyment, knowing the story behind its creation.

May I wish you just as much pleasure on your very own journeys to Wonderland!

Finally, I would like to thank everyone who has helped in the creation of this book: colleagues on *The Mail on Sunday*, my agent, Cat Ledger, and, most of all, my editor, Amanda Li, whose efforts in obtaining all the permissions made the compiling of the Domesday Book look as taxing as the Beano picture crossword.

Frank Barrett

FRANK BARRETT

Editor's note: *The maps in this book are intended as a preliminary guide and as an introduction to each of the locations. We would recommend additional use of detailed maps of each area and road atlases when planning your trips.*

ALICE'S ADVENTURES IN WONDERLAND

by Lewis Carroll

Alice's Adventures in Wonderland is one of those books that everybody thinks they know well, even though they may never have read it. It is full of phrases, rhymes, events and characters that have passed into everyday conversation. Today, you often hear somebody referring to a mad state of affairs as being 'a bit like Alice in Wonderland' or a chaotic occasion being described as resembling 'the Mad Hatter's tea-party'. Phrases from the book such as 'curiouser and curiouser' and 'Off with her head!' are common knowledge.

The events behind the tale of *Alice's Adventures in Wonderland* are every bit as extraordinary as Lewis Carroll's story. Alice was a real girl who went with her sisters on a summer's day picnic trip along the river – and, in a way, she did fall into Wonderland.

★   ★   ★   ★   ★

THE STORY

It is a hot summer's day and Alice and her sister are sitting lazily on a riverbank. Alice is sleepily making a daisy chain. All of a sudden, a White Rabbit runs by, muttering to himself about being late. He then disappears down a hole and Alice decides to follow. She falls down an extremely deep well, landing in an unknown world. And so begin her extraordinary adventures.

After changing in size several times, Alice finds herself in a kitchen where a Duchess is sitting cradling a howling baby and singing to it.

> *Speak roughly to your little boy,*
> *And beat him when he sneezes:*
> *He only does it to annoy,*
> *Because he knows it teases.*

A cook is busy making a cauldron of peppery soup which is making everyone sneeze, and a grinning Cheshire Cat is sitting on the hearth. The Duchess throws the baby about and gives out orders for people's heads to be cut off. Much to Alice's concern, the baby turns into a small pig and trots off.

Alice, illustrated by John Tenniel.

Alice next comes to the March Hare's house, in front of which is a table set for tea; the March Hare, the Hatter and the Dormouse sit at one corner. Alice sits in an armchair and tries to answer their riddles while the Dormouse keeps falling asleep. Eventually, the Hatter's rudeness causes Alice to leave what is '. . . the stupidest tea-party I ever was at in all my life!'

Passing through a door in a tree she finds a large garden, where all the gardeners are painting white roses red. Here Alice meets the King and Queen of Hearts. The Queen is very fond of executions and croquet. After commanding a curious croquet game to take place (the balls are hedgehogs and the mallets are flamingoes) the Queen orders a Gryphon to introduce Alice to a Mock Turtle. The Mock Turtle is sighing pitifully and tells Alice that he is sad because he was once a real turtle. With the Gryphon, he shows her how to dance the Lobster Quadrille.

Suddenly there is a shout in the distance. A trial is beginning! Everyone runs to see it. The Knave of Hearts is standing in chains, accused of stealing tarts, and the King and Queen sit in judgement.

> *The Queen of Hearts, she made some tarts,*
> *All on a summer day:*
> *The Knave of Hearts, he stole those tarts,*
> *And took them quite away!*

In the middle of all this Alice feels herself growing again. While she is being questioned, Alice loses her temper and accuses the whole court of being nothing but a pack of cards! At this they all fly at her. She is half-frightened and half-angry and tries to beat them off. In doing so she finds herself with her head in her sister's lap, brushing away leaves that have fallen from the tree above.

The entire adventure was a strange dream, and Alice tells her sister the whole story. Afterwards, while running in for tea, she thinks her dream was rather wonderful.

★ ★ ★ ★ ★

LEWIS CARROLL

Lewis Carroll is what is known as a pen name – an invented name that a writer uses to disguise his true identity. Lewis Carroll's real name was, in fact, Charles Lutwidge Dodgson.

Charles was born in 1832 in the Cheshire village of Daresbury, the son of a parish priest and the third of 11 children. In 1846 he was sent as a boarder to Rugby, soon to become famous as the setting for *Tom Brown's Schooldays*. Here he demonstrated his great talent for writing by producing a series of home-made magazines. In 1854, Charles graduated from Christ Church College, Oxford, with a first-class degree in mathematics. He then remained at Christ Church as a lecturer, pursuing in his spare time his interest in the newly-discovered art of photography and, of course, his writing. He published numerous articles in humorous magazines, deciding to use the pen name 'Lewis Carroll'.

In 1856 Henry Liddell became the Dean of Christ Church, moving to the college with a son and three daughters: Harry, Lorina, Edith and Alice. Charles soon became friends with the three girls and often photographed them, Alice being a particular favourite. He often took the girls on boat trips on the river and it was as a result of one of these trips that *Alice's Adventures in Wonderland* came to be written. To keep the children entertained, Charles had always to come up with new ideas for stories. On this particular occasion, the heroine of his story was sent 'straight down a rabbit-hole, to begin with, without the least idea what was to happen afterwards'. He called his heroine 'Alice', after Alice Liddell.

According to Charles' own diary, the party did not get back to Christ Church until a quarter past eight. A friend who was also on the trip, Robinson Duckworth, recalled that when the girls were returned to the Deanery, Alice asked Mr Dodgson to write out Alice's adventures for her. This resulted in Charles staying up all night to write out the day's storytelling. But it was not until November 1864, over two years later, that he presented Alice with the completed manuscript. And on 4 July 1865, three years to the day after the famous river trip, Lewis Carroll presented to Alice a special vellum-bound copy of the published book that was soon to make her name famous.

A follow-up title *Through the Looking Glass and What Alice Found There* was published in 1872. Charles continued writing other books but nothing matched the success of the two *Alice* stories, which had become well known all around the world. However, he continued to live a quiet life, never publicly admitting to being the author of *Alice's Adventures in Wonderland*. (Any letters sent to him as 'Lewis Carroll' were returned unopened.)

Charles Dodgson died in Guildford in 1898, aged 66.

THE TOUR

The perfect day for *Alice* lovers would be to re-create that famous outing on the afternoon of 4 July 1862 when *Alice's Adventures in Wonderland* was first dreamt up. Picture the scene that took place in Tom Quad, Christ Church. Under the supervision of their governess, Miss Prickett, three girls emerge from one of the buildings in wide-brimmed hats and flowing white cotton dresses: they are Ina, 13; Alice, 10; and Edith, 8.

Walking into the Old Library, the party heads for the rooms of Charles Lutwidge Dodgson. There they find Mr Dodgson with Robinson Duckworth, both clergymen of the Church of England. Miss Prickett hands the girls over to the safe-keeping of the two men.

The party of five now leaves the college and heads for the river, with the men carrying well-filled picnic baskets. They decide to head upstream towards Godstow, just over three miles away. Drifting sleepily along the river in their rowing boat, the three children beg Charles for a story. In later years, both Charles

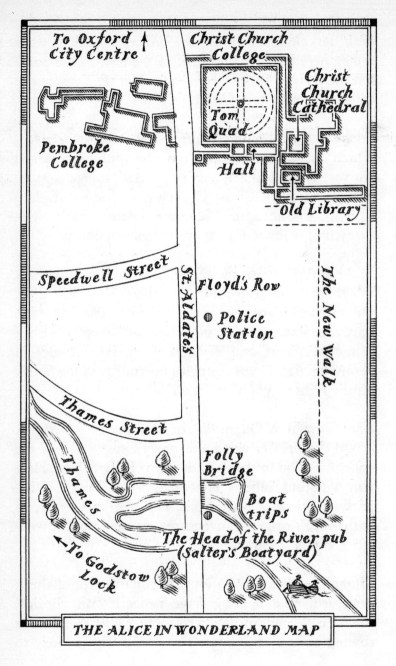

To Oxford City Centre ↑

Christ Church College

Christ Church Cathedral

Pembroke College

Tom Quad

Hall

Old Library

Speedwell Street

St Aldate's

Floyd's Row

Police Station

The New Walk

Thames Street

Thames

Folly Bridge

Boat trips

←To Godstow Lock

The Head of the River pub
(Salter's Boatyard)

THE ALICE IN WONDERLAND MAP

and Alice Liddell recalled this magical summer's day with its cloudless blue sky. Alice Liddell always remembered the blazing heat of the day, as the party left the boat to shelter from the sun in the shadows of some haycocks near Godstow.

For your own *Alice* adventure, start at Christ Church, which is normally open to the public. Oxford University's 'largest and grandest college' (as it describes itself!), Christ Church is a wonderful place to visit. Founded in 1525 and lavishly built, it is everything you would expect an Oxford college to be.

Make sure you visit the fine Hall (the largest old Hall in Oxford) where members of the college still dine. On the walls are portraits of former students who have become famous (including no fewer than 13 Prime Ministers and William Penn, the founder of Pennsylvania). Lewis Carroll's portrait is immediately on the right as you enter the Hall.

Look into Tom Quad, where the famous expedition began, before retracing the party's steps out of the college and on to the road down to Folly Bridge. Here you will find Salter's Boatyard, which is where the party hired their boat from. For your boat trip, as with Alice's original adventure, you will need a well-stocked picnic hamper.

Though boat hire is no longer available from Salter's Boatyard, at a landing stage beneath Folly Bridge, near The Head of the River pub, you can hire a rowing boat by the hour. The round trip is likely to take about six hours. Checking with the boatman which direction to take for Godstow, begin rowing while someone reads from *Alice's Adventures in Wonderland*, starting with the opening verse:

> *All in the golden afternoon*
> *Full leisurely we glide;*
> *For both our oars, with little skill,*
> *By little arms are plied,*
> *While little hands make vain pretence*
> *Our wanderings to guide.*

If you prefer to walk rather than row, the Thames footpath follows the path of the river. If you are not used to rowing, walking may be the better option as it is just over two miles until you reach Port Meadow, with a further mile to Godstow Lock – and remember you will have to row back again!

Once you have found somewhere near Godstow to take your picnic, you can, like Alice at the start of her story, stretch out on the river bank and think about making a daisy chain. If you see the White Rabbit in a waistcoat scampering past, think very carefully before you follow him down his hole . . .

WATERSHIP DOWN
by Richard Adams

Though many successful children's books seem to have curious and unlikely origins, the idea of *Watership Down* started simply enough. It grew out of tales told by Richard Adams to his two small daughters on long car journeys, and, in fact, the book is dedicated to them: 'To Juliet and Rosamond, remembering the road to Stratford-on-Avon'.

The story itself, however, is particularly unusual. It is the saga of a small band of rabbits who, one moonlit night, have to abandon their safe, comfortable warren and search for a new home. But unlike other animal books popular with children, Richard Adams's rabbits were no stuffed toys dressed in blue waistcoats. These were the genuine article, fighting and nobly risking their lives in terrifying fashion.

The book was initially rejected by four publishers and three authors' agents. However, when a small company called Rex Collings eventually brought it out in 1972, it almost overnight became a massive best-seller. It quickly sold over ten million copies and has since been translated into more than 20 languages.

★　　★　　★　　★　　★

THE STORY

*'I don't know what it is,' answered Fiver wretchedly.
'There isn't any danger here, at this moment.
But it's coming – it's coming. Oh, Hazel, look!
The field! It's covered with blood!'*

Fiver is an undersized young rabbit who is also a visionary and can see into the future. A vision of his native warren being savagely destroyed persuades his brother, Hazel, that they should get away while there is still a chance of escape. Fiver and Hazel leave, together with a few other rabbits.

In their ensuing adventures into the unknown, the band are repeatedly saved from danger by the strength and courage of Bigwig and by the intelligence of Blackberry, whose highly-developed powers of thinking help to get them out of tight corners. Dandelion keeps their spirits up with inspiring stories about the rabbit folk hero, El-ahrairah, whose ingenuity always enables him to come out on top, even against the most dangerous enemies.

One of their encounters is with a fine-looking rabbit called Cowslip, who is very welcoming. Life in Cowslip's warren is very sweet. The local farmer makes sure the rabbits are well protected against attack from other animals and generously provides them with delicious food. But when Hazel's group discovers that the price for this happy existence is the constant risk of being snared and killed to

21

provide humans with rabbit meals, they move on at once.

The rabbits' search for a new home continues until they eventually reach Watership Down, where they establish a new warren.

The wind ruffled their fur and tugged at the grass, which smelt of thyme and self-heal. The solitude seemed like a release and a blessing. The height, the sky and the distance went to their heads and they skipped in the sunset.

All is well except for one thing: their little society has no female rabbits and so will not be able to survive for very long.

When Hazel saves the life of Kehaar, a seagull, the grateful bird in return inspects the surrounding area from the skies. Kehaar establishes that there is a large warren, not too far away, which has many extra females. Hazel's approaches are rudely rejected, as the warren is under the leadership of General Woundwort, a mad rabbit dictator. Eventually, Hazel's rabbits manage to free some does, defeating General Woundwort and his troops in a final battle of ingenuity. Watership Down survives as a happy and content warren.

(Hazel) lived a tidy few summers – as they say in that part of the world – and learned to know well the changes of the downs to spring, to winter and to spring again. He saw more young rabbits than

he could remember. And sometimes, when they
told tales on a sunny evening by the beech trees,
he could not clearly recall whether they were
about himself or about some other rabbit hero
of days gone by.

★   ★   ★   ★   ★

RICHARD ADAMS

While Watership Down might sound like a made-up location, such as Narnia or Neverland, it is in fact a real place on the edge of Newbury in the heart of the English countryside. From the house where he was brought up, the young Richard Adams could gaze from his window towards the real Watership Down. Little did he guess that it would provide him with the setting for one of the best-loved stories of the century.

Richard Adams was born in 1920 and had a very contented up-bringing. His father, a doctor with a country practice, was a devoted amateur naturalist. While many people would be content to know the names of the more common birds and the songs they sung, Mr Adams was keen to show that he could distinguish between less common varieties like the blackcap and the garden warbler. He taught his son the names of many birds and flowers, and Richard came to inherit his father's desire to know and understand the natural world. This love of nature meant that when, in later life, Richard wrote a book about rabbits, he was to make it as rabbit-like as he could.

23

And this was the secret of the success of *Watership Down*.

Richard Adams went from public school to Oxford University, and then immediately into the army. It was here that he gained the sense of fellowship and adventure which binds together the animal characters of *Watership Down*.

After the Second World War, Richard Adams joined the Civil Service, writing *Watership Down* at night after returning home from his job. His aim was to write 'a proper grown-up novel for children'. After 25 years at the Department of the Environment, the huge success of *Watership Down* allowed Richard Adams to become a full-time writer. He followed this book with other popular novels, including *Shardik* and *The Plague Dogs*.

THE TOUR

Watership Down is almost unique among the books featured in this guide, as it actually contains a map of the action. While this is designed to help you follow the progress of the story – it is also very useful for anyone who wants to walk the *Watership Down* trail.

Unless you are an exceptionally keen walker, you will probably not want to cover the entire distance tackled by Hazel and his fellow rabbits – a total of around 12

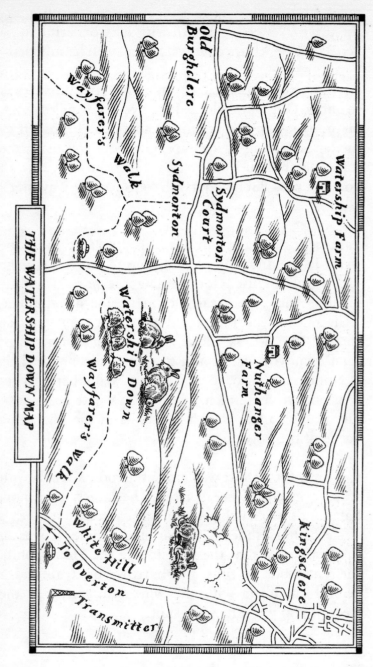

THE WATERSHIP DOWN MAP

Old Burghclere

Wayfarer's Walk

Sydmonton

Sydmonton Court

Watership Farm

Watership Down

Wayfarer's Walk

Nuthanger Farm

White Hill

To Overton Transmitter

Kingsclere

miles from beginning to end. A bracing stroll along the top of Watership Down with its wonderful views across the Berkshire countryside may well be sufficient.

Driving from Kingsclere, take the road that runs towards Old Burghclere. Just over two miles west, before reaching Sydmonton, a small road runs off to the left, climbing Watership Down. As you reach the top of the hill, just over half a mile from the turn-off, you will pass Public Footpath signs for the Wayfarer's Walk.

Park near the signs and head eastwards up the slope (back in the direction of Kingsclere). You will emerge on to gallops used for training racehorses, with a stunning view. You really feel as if you are standing right on top of the world and that you can see forever. If you look about a mile and a half north of the Down, you will be able to spot a farm house. This is Nuthanger Farm, to which Hazel led a party to get four does from a hutch. This is also where he went to lure a dog to help save the rabbits in the final, epic battle of the book.

Continue for a short way along the footpath until you reach a group of beech trees. The largest tree, now half cut down, has Bigwig's name carved on it, with a circle of horseshoes nailed around a hole. It was in this leafy area that the rabbits dug the Honeycomb, their network of runs and burrows built around a central chamber. With the wind whispering in the trees, it really is a magical spot.

For a longer walk to Watership Down, begin the Wayfarer's Walk footpath from the White Hill car park. You will find this on the B3051 Kingsclere to Overton road, near a large transmitter mast. The walk from White Hill to Watership Down is about five miles there and back – the view is stunning and the fresh air superb.

Whichever walk you choose, keep a close watch and you may even spot a rabbit or two!

THOMAS THE TANK ENGINE

by The Reverend W Awdry

A steam engine has always got character
– it's the most human of all man-made machines.

Anyone who has ever stood on a station platform and watched a steam locomotive go hissing by will know exactly what the Reverend Awdry means – steam trains are living, breathing creatures. And when Reverend Awdry began his railway stories in 1943, steam trains were as common and familiar as buses are today. And through his captivating characters and charming storytelling, the *Thomas the Tank Engine* tales are still enjoyed today, long after the demise of steam. Each succeeding generation has been won over by the stories about the cheerful little engine and his friends and, since being made into a television programme just over 12 years ago (with narration by ex-Beatle Ringo Starr), the tales have hit new heights of popularity right around the world.

Thomas and friends, illustrated by John Kenney.

THE STORY

The Island of Sodor is the home of Sir Topham Hatt's railway and its Really Useful Engines. Sir Topham Hatt, the Fat Controller, is a firm yet kindly character who has the power to punish or reward the engines. His timetables must be followed, the lines kept to and all signals obeyed. Each of the engines, just like people, has its own character.

Thomas himself is a 'cheeky little engine' with a child-like personality.

. . . he used to play tricks on them. He liked best of all to come quietly beside a big engine dozing on a siding and make him jump.

Henry, with his green paintwork and red stripes, is very fine looking. But he is a grumpy and disobedient engine who one day ends up being bricked up in a tunnel when he refuses to go out in the rain. Another day, when Henry is ill, Thomas is given a chance to pull Henry's passenger train. Unfortunately however, he starts off before the crew can couple him on to the train. Dashing off without the coaches makes the passengers angry and gets Thomas into trouble with the Fat Controller.

Gordon is a big and proud engine who usually pulls the express.

'Poop, poop, poop. Hurry up, you,' said Gordon, crossly. 'Peep, pip, peep. Hurry yourself,' said cheeky Thomas.

One day, however, pride comes before a fall when Gordon has to take the goods train out. He says this makes him ashamed, but a worse indignity is to follow. He gets stuck half-way up a hill and little Edward has to save the day.

James is a middle-sized red engine with yellow stripes, who we first meet hurtling along with his brake blocks on fire. It's up to Thomas to rescue him, after he ends up in a field of cows.

In the early stories, Thomas is always pulling empty coaches so that the big engines can go and rest. We are delighted for him when at last he is given his own branch line.

Now Thomas is as happy as can be. He has a branch line all to himself, and puffs proudly backwards and forwards with two coaches all day.

★　　★　　★　　★　　★

THE REVEREND W AWDRY

Wilbert Awdry O.B.E. was born near Romsey, Hampshire in 1911. His father, Reverend Vere Awdry, was a train-lover who founded The Ampfield Model Railway: a generously-proportioned model railway layout which ran for 40 yards in the vicarage garden.

In 1917 the Awdry family moved to Box, a fortunate place for train-lovers. The Box Tunnel had been built here in 1841 by Isambard Kingdom Brunel for the Great Western Railway, and Vere could look through a telescope and note down which engines were passing by. Lying in his bed at night young Wilbert could hear the trains coming and going into Box station, particularly the heavy freight trains that needed the assistance of a tank engine to get up the gradient.

I would hear them snorting up the grade and little imagination was needed to hear in the puffings and pantings of the two engines the conversation they were having with one another:
'I can't do it! I can't do it! I can't do it.'
'Yes, you can! Yes, you can! Yes, you can!'

After graduating from Oxford University, Wilbert decided to follow his father into the clergy. He began in 1936 as curate at All Saints, Odiham in Hampshire, though after marrying and having a child, Christopher (born in 1940), Wilbert moved to King's Norton near Birmingham. It was here that the family were living when Christopher caught the measles, and Wilbert made up a tale to amuse his sick son. There was a poem about trains that Christopher particularly enjoyed, and Wilbert decided to illustrate it, drawing little faces on the trains for fun: one smiling, one cross, one sad. Two-year-old Christopher immediately wanted to know why the sad one looked gloomy, and Wilbert replied that it was because he was old and hadn't been out for a long time. The engine's name, he told Christopher, was Edward, and after further prompting, he went on to devise the story of *Edward's Day Out*. In the next story he made up, Gordon appeared, while in a third, Henry made his entry. These three stories were told again and again – and eventually Wilbert wrote them down as his long-running series, *The Three Railway Engines*. As an adult, Christopher Awdry continued the family tradition and has written the *Thomas* stories since 1984, including books 26-40 in the Railway series.

It was Wilbert's wife, Margaret, who decided that the stories were good enough to be published, and after several disappointments, they were accepted by Edmund Ward for £25 and published in one book to huge acclaim. Wilbert then began a fourth railway book, *Thomas Races Bertie The Bus*, introducing his star, Thomas the Tank Engine. His children, Christopher, Hilary and Veronica, immediately protested that the contest wasn't fair because Bertie had to deal with a variety of hazards such as traffic lights and level crossing gates while Thomas sailed gaily through. To prove that it was an even race, Wilbert drew a map to show road and railway line and the obstacles on each. The map quickly grew to include the locations of other stories.

Now Wilbert needed a name for the locations on his map. In 1950, on a visit to the Isle of Man, he found the answer. He discovered that the local bishop was called the Bishop of Sodor and Man. 'Sodor' came from an ancient word, the Sudreys, used to refer to the islands west of Scotland. There was no actual place called Sodor – so Wilbert created his own Island of Sodor, lying between Barrow-in-Furness on the English mainland and the Isle of Man. He even wrote a guide to its people, history and railways.

The Reverend Wilbert Awdry passed away peacefully on 21 March 1997 at the age of 85.

THE TOUR

The Island of Sodor may not actually exist, but don't let this small detail deter you from trying to find it. True Thomas pilgrims will want to visit Barrow, one of the real places frequented by the Reverend Awdry's engines. The wonderful countryside of the surrounding Lake District also provides an alluring array of great little railways for that authentic *Thomas the Tank Engine* experience.

After driving through ravishing countryside, most noticeable as you drive into Barrow-in-Furness are the huge sheds which were constructed by Vickers for the building of the Polaris and Trident nuclear submarines. Barrow's excellent Dock Museum offers a wealth of intriguing history on the port's shipbuilding industry, and look out for the working men's club in Abbey Road, modelled on a Picardy chateau. It is the Vickers works which no doubt inspired the Vicarstown of the books, where Gordon overshot the turntable. Just beyond Vicarstown, on a clear day, you might catch a glimpse of The Ballahoo Tunnels, famous as the spot where unhappy Henry was bricked up.

If by now you are yearning for a whiff of steam and the roar of the engine, this part of the Lake District offers a couple of top-class steam railway lines. The Lakeside & Haverthwaite Railway at Haverthwaite Station, near Ulverston, offers a lovely ride up the beautiful Leven Valley via Newby Bridge to Lakeside. Here you can connect with Bowness and Ambleside on the Windermere steamers. But perhaps the best known of the area's steam railways is the Ravenglass & Eskdale Railway – 'L'aal Ratty' – which claims to be England's oldest narrow-gauge railway. This was the inspiration for several books in Reverend Awdry's Railway series. The railway runs for seven miles from the Irish Sea to the foot of Lakeland's highest fells, through countryside which Thomas and his friends would think looked just like home.

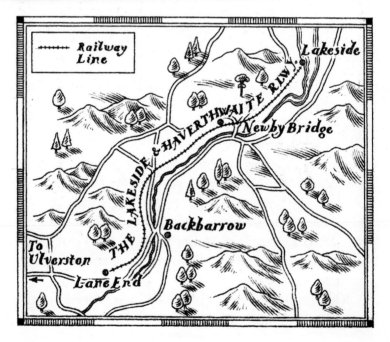

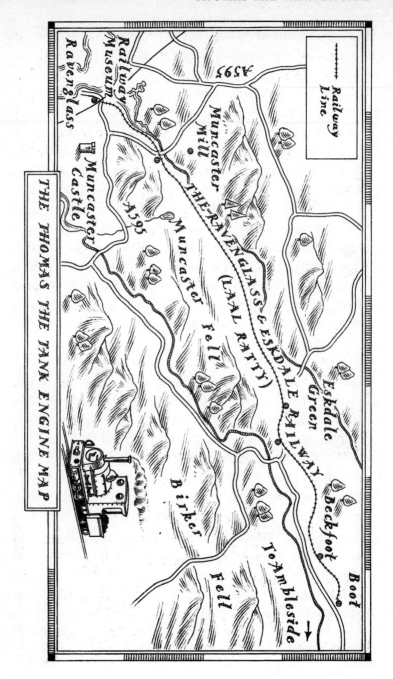

THE THOMAS THE TANK ENGINE MAP

Ravenglass
Railway Museum
Muncaster Mill
A595
Muncaster Castle
A595
Muncaster Fell
THE RAVENGLASS & ESKDALE RAILWAY
(LAAL RATTY)
Eskdale Green
Beckfoot
Boot
Birker Fell
To Ambleside

Railway Line

PETER PAN
by J M Barrie

Peter Pan, the story of the boy who never grew up, is one of the best-known children's stories of the past 100 years. Still avidly read, there have been many adaptations of this firm favourite. First performed as a play at the Duke of York's Theatre in London on 27 December 1904, *Peter Pan* has been performed every Christmas since in pantomime. It has also been made into an animated film by Walt Disney and filmed more recently as the live action *Hook* by Stephen Spielberg.

The tale itself is pure fantasy, centring on a boy who never grows up and who flies with fairies, and telling of lost children who live underground, of warring Red Indians and pirates, and of a crocodile which has swallowed an alarm clock. But while you may not be able to follow Peter and Wendy to Neverland, with the aid of a London street guide you can track down real places intimately connected with the Darling family and their adventures. And you will find that the story behind the writing of *Peter Pan* is even more strange and poignant than the fiction.

THE STORY

All children, except one, grow up.

Peter Pan, a magical boy who never gets older, comes one night to the nursery of the Darling children: Wendy, John and Michael. He teaches them how to fly and directs them through the skies to his home:

Second to the right, and straight on till morning.

Neverland is a country full of the most exciting elements from children's stories: Red Indians, mermaids, wolves, and most importantly of all, pirates. The pirates' leader is Captain Hook, named after the steel hook he wears instead of a right hand. This hand was bitten off by a crocodile, who, as Hook explains:

. . . liked my arm so much . . .
that it has followed me ever since . . .
licking its lips for the rest of me . . .

Hook and Peter are old enemies, and the Darling children are rapidly caught up in the rivals' struggle. The evil Hook tries to poison Peter, also nearly killing Peter's mischievous fairy friend, Tinker Bell. Finally, he takes Wendy and her brothers prisoner, together with the 'Lost Boys' who live with Peter.

After a great battle, Hook is eaten by the crocodile who has been searching for him for so long. Wendy, John and Michael return home, where they are reunited with their parents and Nana, their nursemaid and guard-dog. However, every spring, Wendy goes back to Neverland to do Peter's spring-cleaning for him in the little house he and the Lost Boys once built for her in the tree-tops.

J M BARRIE

Sir James Barrie was born in 1860 in the village of Kirriemuir, near Dundee in Scotland. The son of a handloom weaver, he adored his mother, whom he wrote about fondly in later life. After an education at Dumfries and Edinburgh University, he embarked on a career in newspapers, starting work in 1888 on *The Nottinghamshire Journal*. However in the same year, Barrie started to write in his spare time, and so began the start of his highly-successful career.

Other adults may have considered Barrie odd: he was only five foot tall, had a large walrus moustache, and dressed in a bowler hat and an outsize overcoat. But children always found him thoroughly delightful. Margaret Henley, who died aged just six, referred to Barrie as 'my friendy', which in her childish lisp she pronounced as 'my wendy'. When Barrie needed a name for his *Peter Pan* heroine he called her Wendy and in the process invented a brand new Christian name.

In 1894, Barrie married the actress Mary Ansell, settling in London at 133 Gloucester Road. They had no children of their own, though they did have a large

St Bernard dog, Porthos – the model for 'Nana' in *Peter Pan*. It was on one of Barrie's regular walks with Porthos to Kensington Gardens that he first met a five-year-old boy called George Llewelyn Davies, his brother Jack and their baby brother Peter. Barrie used to enthrall the boys with stirring tales of fairies, pirates, hangings and desert islands, out of which the *Peter Pan* story gradually took shape. (It underwent many transformations before finally becoming the tale we know and love today.) The Llewelyn family (which later numbered five boys) was, of course, subtly remoulded in fiction as the Darling family.

J M Barrie became the official guardian of the Llewelyn boys when their mother, Sylvia, died in 1910. (Arthur, their father, had died in 1907.) Due to the success of his writing, Barrie was later made a baronet and received several honorary degrees.

J M Barrie died in 1937 and was buried close to his parents in the local cemetery at Kirriemuir.

THE TOUR

It is well worth visiting J M Barrie's birthplace at 9 Brechin Road, Kirriemuir, near Dundee, which is now a museum. You can still see the little wash house at the back where the young Barrie staged his first plays. However, it was in London that J M Barrie won his success, first becoming well-known for his stories of everyday Scottish life, then achieving fame in both

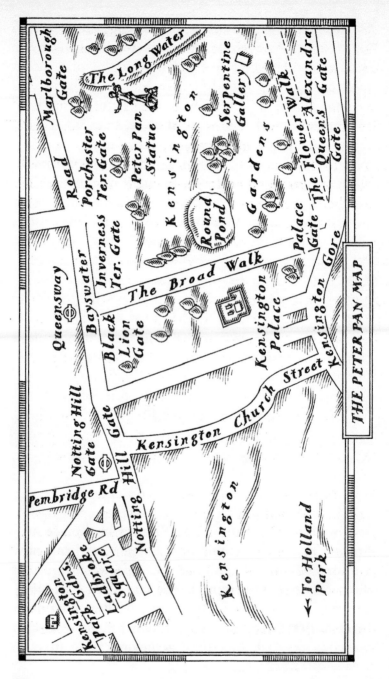

THE PETER PAN MAP

40

Britain and America as a playwright, and finally becoming a household name around the world because of the success of *Peter Pan*.

Start the trail at J M Barrie's home at 133 Gloucester Road, a short walk south from Gloucester Road tube station. As you stand outside, travel back in your mind to the turn of the century and imagine the small figure of Barrie and his larger-than-life dog embarking on their regular expedition northwards up the Gloucester Road to Kensington Gardens.

Next, less than ten minutes' walk from Notting Hill Gate tube station, wander down to the former home of the Llewelyn Davies family at 31 Kensington Park Gardens. The house is clearly the one that Barrie describes as the home of the Darling family. It is a curious feeling to stand outside and think that it was here, at an upstairs window, that Peter Pan was parted from his shadow by Nana the dog. And it was from this same window, while the Darlings were dining at Number 27 (two doors down!), that Peter, Wendy, John and Michael made their flight to Neverland.

Now take the walk that the Davies children, in the company of their nurse, would have taken regularly to Kensington Gardens. The Notting Hill/North Kensington area that you will pass through is one of the grandest parts of London, fascinating for its elegant houses, but rarely visited by tourists. Walking here after twilight, looking at the cosy families at their firesides, it is easy to imagine how the motherless Peter Pan would have looked on longingly.

Once in Kensington Gardens, head for the top end of the Serpentine where you will find a statue of Peter Pan himself. This was commissioned and paid for by Barrie who had it erected in secret on the night of 30 April 1912: he wanted children to believe that it had arrived by magic. Barrie was, in fact, disappointed with the statue. He wanted it modelled on Michael Llewelyn Davies, but the sculptor Sir George Frampton used another model.

The final destination on the *Peter Pan* trail is Great Ormond Street Hospital, near Russell Square tube station. By special arrangement with the hospital's archivist you can visit the *Peter Pan* Gallery and look at the hospital's collection of *Peter Pan* memorabilia. The hospital's links with the tale of the magical boy began in 1929, when J M Barrie was approached for financial help by the hospital's board and granted the hospital the benefits of the *Peter Pan* copyright. This should have expired in 1987, 50 years after Barrie's death, but thanks to the help of Lord and Lady Callaghan, the hospital benefits from *Peter Pan* in perpetuity. It was a condition of Barrie's gift to the hospital that the actual amount of money it generated should never be made public. The hospital will only say that it is the single most generous gift it has ever been given, which means that it has so far been worth many millions.

And so *Peter Pan* has ceased to be a remote work of fiction. Barrie's story has become a gift of good health to succeeding generations – surely the very best sort of fairy tale.

LORNA DOONE
by R D Blackmore

orna Doone is one of the great romantic stories of
English writing. Nowadays we tend to think that
a romance is simply a love story. However, a true
romantic novel is a great adventure story where, after
extraordinary deeds, the hero triumphs over the evil
villain and, of course, marries his sweetheart.

Lorna Doone has all of this and much more. The
story is set in England, shortly after the Great Fire of
London. It tells of highwaymen and their dark deeds
on Exmoor, furious fights to the death, and forbidden
love, culminating in a tense, nail-biting ending when
it looks as if the villain may finally triumph.

Based on Devonshire folklore, one of the great
attractions of the book is that many of the places it
describes are real. They can still be found in or around
the marvellous countryside of Exmoor, little changed
from when Blackmore wrote about them over 100
years ago.

★　　★　　★　　★　　★

THE STORY

The book centres on the doings of the lawless Doone
family, beginning with their murder of Jan Ridd's

father. A day later, while out fishing, Jan Ridd strays by chance into Doone Valley, and nearly drowns. He falls unconscious, waking up to the sight of Lorna bending over him and caring for him. Lorna helps him to escape from the valley through a secret entrance, and the picture of her face never leaves his mind.

I had never heard so sweet a sound as came from between her bright red lips, while there she knelt and gazed at me; neither had I ever seen anything so beautiful as the large dark eyes intent upon me, full of pity and wonder. And then . . . I wandered with my hazy eyes down the black shower of her hair, as to my jaded gaze it seemed; and where it fell on the turf, among it . . . was the first primrose of the season. And since that day, I think of her, through all the rough storms of my life, when I see an early primrose.

Seven years later they meet again and their secret and dangerous romance begins.

When Sir Ensor Doone dies, Lorna is left unprotected. Jan decides to rescue her. During a great snowstorm he carries her away to his farm and so saves her from a forced marriage to Carver Doone. It is discovered, however, that Lorna is not a real Doone but is from the rich Scottish Dugal family. Her high birth and new wealth mean that a marriage with Jan, a farmer, would be unfitting. Fortunately Jan wins the favour of King James II – who makes him Sir Jan Ridd – and his marriage to Lorna is approved.

Regardless, the Doones continue their reign of terror. Led by Jan, the people of Exmoor decide to strike against the Doones and storm Doone Valley – only Carver Doone escapes.

Shortly afterwards Jan and Lorna stand joyfully at the altar of Oare Church, about to be married.

Lorna's dress was of pure white, clouded with faint lavender . . . and as simple as need be, except for the perfect loveliness.

But their happiness is cut short when Lorna is shot during the service by Carver Doone. Jan immediately rides in pursuit, determined to avenge the attack on Lorna which he believes has left her dead . . .

Darling eyes, the clearest eyes, the loveliest, the most loving eyes – the sound of a shot rang through the church, and those eyes were dim with death.

★ ★ ★ ★ ★

R D BLACKMORE

Richard Dodderidge Blackmore was born in Longworth, North Berkshire, in 1825. Following an outbreak of typhoid fever which killed his mother, the family moved to Culmstock in East Devon where his father was appointed curate. (His father's side of the family had lived in Devon for many generations.) It was while growing up in Devon that Blackmore would have learnt the 17th century legend of the lawless Doone family.

Like the hero of *Lorna Doone*, Blackmore was sent to Blundell's school in Tiverton and then to Exeter College, Oxford. He embarked on a career as a lawyer but, after illness, he gave this up and spent some years teaching. He later moved to Teddington, west of London, living as a market gardener, growing fruit and vegetables.

To help make ends meet, Blackmore took up writing. In 40 years he published 14 novels and seven volumes of poetry – but of all his writing, *Lorna Doone* remains the only well-known book. While writing it, Blackmore toured Devon and Somerset, revisiting the places he talks about in the book, interviewing local people, and learning more about the extraordinary story of the fearsome Doones. However, though the book is today considered a classic, it was not instantly successful on first publication: of the first 500 copies printed, only 300 were sold.

R D Blackmore died on 20 January 1900 in London.

THE TOUR

Blackmore so vividly describes Doone Valley, its surrounding countryside and wildlife, that it is tremendously exciting to see it at first hand. There are two trails you can walk, which trace the story of Lorna Doone and Jan Ridd in dramatic fashion.

Both walks can be started at Malmsmead, where a

17th century packhorse bridge spans Badgworthy Water. Following the path that runs alongside it, you will pass the Blackmore Memorial, a standing stone. From here you can continue to Lank Combe Water – which in the novel is the terrifying Waterslide. It's here that Jan first meets Lorna after fishing for loaches, when he almost drowns. Although in reality the Waterslide is much smaller than Blackmore suggests in the book, it's still thrilling to be able to find small loaches under the stones, or to see an early primrose – which always so reminded Jan of Lorna.

Along the path from Badgworthy Wood and the Waterslide is Hoccombe Combe. This is the site of the medieval hermitage of Badgworthy. When the Doones settled in the uninhabited Royal Forest of Exmoor, the only houses available to them were those that had formed this deserted village. Today, the remaining mounds will give you an idea of the ground plan that Blackmore knew and imagined built up so grandly in his fiction. This dreaded valley of the Doones, the outlaws' stronghold, is as spooky in real life as it is in the book – 'not a single house stood there but was the home of murder'.

Further along the trail you will come upon Lorna Doone Farm. No description in the novel fits any known building exactly, but this building may have been the model for Jan Ridd's Plovers Barrow Farm. Though it doesn't look exactly as Blackmore describes it, it certainly has the 'strong, dark mountain' behind it and the stream in front.

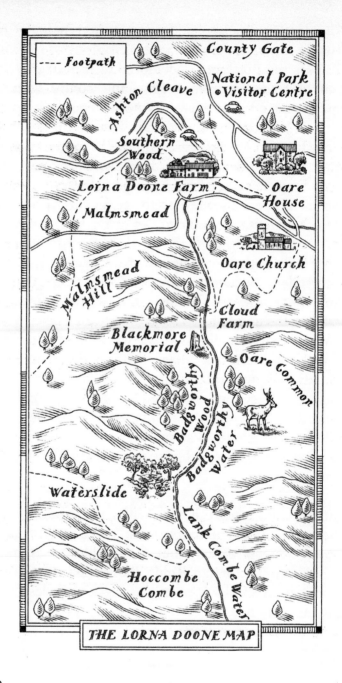

THE LORNA DOONE MAP

Another farmhouse which bears similarities to the description of Jan Ridd's home is Oare House. This is further along the trail and can be seen from the 18th century bridge over Oare Water. As described in the novel, at Oare House the land becomes more sheltered and the desolate moor seems far away. Also, Jan is able to see his father's grave in the churchyard from his home and this he certainly could have done from Oare House, as Oare Church is nearby.

Here in the church, where the story reaches its thrilling climax, things have changed little since Blackmore described it. It is small, dark and atmospheric. Close your eyes and you can almost see Lorna in her dress of pure white and Jan, her bridegroom. It was through a small side window in this church (a sign shows which one) that Lorna was shot by Carver. In the still quiet of the place you almost expect to see his face peering in and hear the shot ring out.

FURTHER INFORMATION

The Exmoor National Park has devised two walks through 'Doone Country', one short (0.5km) and one longer (4km). Both are clearly set out in a leaflet, available from local visitor centres. You may also find it helpful to contact Visitor Services, Exmoor National Park, Exmoor House, Dulverton, Somerset, TA22 9HL.
A guidebook called *The Lorna Doone Trail* (Exmoor Press) by S H Burton offers interesting background information and is available from local visitor centres.

THE SECRET GARDEN
by Frances Hodgson Burnett

When people are asked to name the book they most enjoyed when they were young, a surprisingly large number are quick to recall the very special pleasure of reading *The Secret Garden*. Published in 1911, this classic children's book has many magic ingredients. However, the two main characters are most unsympathetic. Mary, an orphan, is spoilt and very badly-behaved.

> *. . . everybody said she was the most disagreeable-looking child ever seen. It was true, too. She had a little thin face and a little thin body, thin light hair and a sour expression . . . She was not an affectionate child and had never cared much for anyone.*

The bed-ridden Colin is even more spoilt and is given to fearful temper tantrums. 'He could have anything he asked for and was never made to do anything he did not like to do.' Being an invalid gives him an excuse to misbehave, as no one dares get angry.

Through the story we see how both characters change, becoming better and nicer people through helping each other, and by discovering together the delights of nature in their secret garden.

THE STORY

Mary Lennox is orphaned in India when her parents die of cholera. She is sent home to England to live with an uncle she has never met, in his great lonely house on the Yorkshire moors. Initially she is a spoilt and disagreeable girl with a 'quite contrary expression', though the fresh air and the companionship of two plain-speaking Yorkshire characters – Martha the housemaid and Ben Weatherstaff the gardener – help Mary transform herself into a friendly, healthy girl.

One day, while out playing in the grounds, she discovers a hidden doorway to the mysterious secret garden which has been shut up for 10 years since the death of her uncle's wife.

> *. . . it was different from any other place she had ever seen in her life.*

Without telling anyone she begins gardening there and, magically, her life seems to brighten up in many ways. She meets Dickon, Martha's younger brother, who helps her with the garden and seems to have uncanny powers over birds, animals and plants. Dickon becomes a good friend.

Mary eventually discovers the other secret her uncle's house holds – her guardian's son. Colin is confined to bed, convinced he is going to die. But Mary succeeds where everyone else has failed. She braves Colin's tantrums and persuades him (though somewhat harshly) to try to lead a normal life.

Because she was the stronger of the two, she was beginning to get the better of him. The truth was that he never had a fight with anyone like himself in his life, and, upon the whole, it was rather good for him, though neither he nor Mary knew anything about that.

From then on, Colin, Mary and Dickon share the magic of the secret garden. Colin's strength grows. He even learns how to walk again and becomes confident that he is well.

Mary! Dickon! I shall get well! And I shall live for ever and ever and ever!

When Colin's father finally returns home from abroad, Colin runs to greet him, full of health. He tells him about the secret garden and what it has meant to him, and that he will never need his wheel-chair again.

★　★　★　★　★

FRANCES HODGSON BURNETT

The story of Mrs Burnett's life is every bit as extra-ordinary as the plots of her books (others include *Little Lord Fauntleroy* and *A Little Princess*), in which children suddenly find themselves in changed and difficult circumstances.

Mrs Burnett was born Frances Eliza Hodgson in 1849, the daughter of a wealthy Manchester iron-monger. She grew up one of five children in a comfortable house in an area at the heart of the Industrial Revolution, surrounded by the poverty of the families living in the slums nearby. Her father's death, when Frances was just three, marked the beginning of the end of the good life for her own family. Her mother was eventually forced to sell the business and in 1865, when Frances was 15, the family decided to emigrate to America.

Frances's mother took the family to Tennessee, where her brother ran a grocery store in the town of Knoxville. But they were always short of money and life was difficult. The children devised a range of money-making schemes such as giving music lessons and breeding chickens, and it was with the idea of earning some extra cash that Frances put her talent for storytelling to profitable use by writing for magazines. She sold her first magazine story when she was just 17.

When Frances was 20 her mother died and she found herself responsible for the family. This forced her to turn out magazine stories at a faster and faster rate, bringing her extraordinary success. By the age of just 23, she had earned enough money to travel back to England for a holiday. On her return she married Swan Burnett, a physician who was to become a leading eye and ear specialist. After living in Paris for a time and giving birth to two children, Mrs Burnett began writing novels. In 1877, her first book *That*

Lass o'Lowrie's (which used her childhood memories of Lancashire) was an instant hit in America and Britain. Her biggest success came eight years later with *Little Lord Fauntleroy*, whose main character she based on her younger son, Vivian. Helped by a stage version, the book became one of the most popular in America, and Mrs Burnett found herself an international celebrity as a result.

On separating from her husband, Frances began to spend more time in Britain, renting Maytham Hall in the village of Rolvenden, Kent, in 1898. It was here that for the first time she had the chance to enjoy gardening, her Rose Garden being in many respects the 'secret garden' itself.

When it was published in 1911, *The Secret Garden* was not an instant success. Its popularity ever since suggests that it was ahead of its time in its style.

Frances Hodgson Burnett died at her house in Long Island near New York on 29 October 1924, four weeks before her 75th birthday.

THE TOUR

The inspiration for Frances Hodgson Burnett's best-loved book still survives and is open to the public, but her 'secret garden' remains very much a secret. You will not find the information advertised in a tourist board leaflet nor set out in any guide book.

From 1898 to 1907, the author's home in England was Maytham Hall in Rolvenden, three miles from Tenterden, in Kent. Arriving through lovely undulating fields, dotted with the distinctive oast houses, it is easy to see why Mrs Burnett was attracted to Rolvenden, with its brick and weatherboarded houses and wide village street. Heading south through the village on the A28, turn left at the church of St Mary the Virgin and follow Maytham Road for about 400 yards down to Maytham Hall.

The house that Mrs Burnett knew burnt down shortly after she gave up the tenancy. The house you see now was designed by the distinguished architect Sir Edwin Lutyens. The layout of the gardens, however, is more or less as it was when Mrs Burnett was there. The walled garden was in the Rose Garden, where Mrs Burnett used to sit in a white dress and large hat and write. (The gazebo which she used is still there.) It was here she first had the idea for *The Secret Garden* when she befriended a robin which would take crumbs from her hand.

When Mrs Burnett had first arrived at the house, she had found the Rose Garden overgrown and unkempt. A low arched gateway led to a garden strewn with weeds and thorns. That gateway has since been bricked up, though you can still see the shape of the old doorway on the far end of the west wall. The new gate, designed by Lutyens, is just around the corner. Step through and you can share Mary Lennox's excitement when she entered the fictional garden.

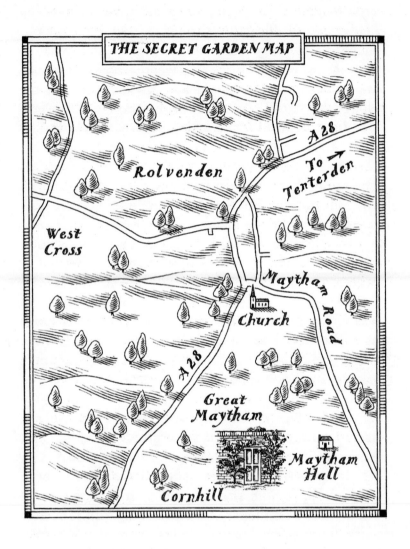

She was standing inside the secret garden . . . It was the sweetest, most mysterious-looking place anyone could imagine. The high walls which shut it in were covered with the leafless stems of climbing roses, which were so thick they were matted together.

The garden is a lot neater and much more orderly today but you can still feel some of the mystery which must have infected Mrs Burnett all those years ago.

After exploring the garden, retrace your path back to the Church of St Mary the Virgin. On entering, look down on the bottom right-hand side of the nave and you will see a tablet, made by Tiffany's New York after Mrs Burnett's death. It reads: 'In memory of Frances Hodgson Burnett for some time tenant of Maytham Hall. "Careful to maintain good works," Titus 3.8.'

In 1993 a film version of *The Secret Garden* was shot, the locations of which you can also visit. Misselthwaite Manor was played partly by Fountains Abbey near Ripon in Yorkshire and partly by Allerton Park, a Gothic revival mansion just outside Knaresborough in North Yorkshire. The town of Knaresborough was used as Misselthwaite.

FURTHER INFORMATION

Please note that Maytham Hall is now a private house, owned by the Country Houses Association and divided into flats for use by elderly people. It is advisable to contact the Hall before visiting as admission is only allowed at certain times through the year.

DANNY, THE CHAMPION OF THE WORLD

by Roald Dahl

Of all children's writers, probably none has been more controversial or more outspoken than Roald Dahl. While children adore his books, many adults have accused them of being 'unsuitable', condemning them for cruel storylines and the unflattering way in which women are often presented. For instance, in *George's Marvellous Medicine*, a boy poisons his bad-tempered grandmother with toilet cleaner. And *The Witches* was banned from schools in America because parents said it either frightened their children or encouraged an interest in the occult. But Dahl himself, who regarded adults as 'the enemy' of children, remained sceptical about interpretations such as these and only took notice of his most important audience – the children themselves.

Despite his death in 1990, Roald Dahl's success shows no sign of coming to an end. With successful new American film versions of *James and the Giant Peach* and *Matilda*, he remains as popular as ever.

THE STORY

Since Danny was four months old, when his mother died, his father has looked after him. They think the world of each other and have a life together which is cosy and secure, but most of all, fun. They live in a small gipsy caravan, sleeping in bunks and having regular midnight feasts of steaming cups of cocoa and cheese sandwiches. His father weaves wonderful tales every night before Danny goes to sleep.

I really loved living in that gipsy caravan . . . when I was tucked up in my bunk and my father was telling me stories . . . Most wonderful of all was the feeling that when I went to sleep, my father would still be

Danny, illustrated by Quentin Blake.

59

> *there, very close to me, sitting in his chair by the*
> *fire, or lying in the bunk above my own.*

Life with Danny's father is exciting and magical. He
owns a garage and filling station and, by the age of
seven, Danny can take an engine apart and put it back
together – pistons, crankshaft and all. Danny's father
shows him how to build a kite, make a fire-balloon,
and much more.

One night, after his ninth birthday, Danny wakes up
to find that his father isn't in the caravan or the workshop. As he sits and waits, for the first time in his life,
he feels the first stirrings of panic. Eventually his
father arrives home and shares a dark and
shocking secret. He has been poaching pheasants, just
as his father did before him. He tells Danny the secret
methods he uses, including the most amazing fact of
all – that pheasants adore raisins. Danny's father
poaches on the land of the rich brewer Mr Hazell, a
thoroughly unlikeable man for whom we have little
sympathy.

> *Mr Victor Hazell was a roaring snob and he tried*
> *desperately to get in with what he believed were the*
> *right kind of people. He hunted with the hounds and*
> *gave shooting parties and wore fancy waistcoats.*

One night, when Danny's father is poaching, he falls
into a pit – a trap dug by Mr Hazell's keepers – and
breaks his ankle. Danny has to come to the rescue by
driving a Baby Austin from the workshop, though he's

almost caught by the police in the process. His father wants to pay Mr Hazell back by sabotaging the start of the shooting season. This is when Danny comes up with his champion idea to rid Mr Hazell's land of pheasants, robbing his rich guests of their sport.

And we shall call this method 'The Sleeping Beauty'.
It will be a landmark in the history of poaching!

Danny and his father stuff raisins with sleeping tablets and go to Hazell Wood together at sunset, before the pheasants go up in the trees to roost. They scatter the drugged raisins in the clearing, right under the keepers' nose. Later. . . thump, thump, thump! Nearly 200 pheasants fall to the ground, fast asleep and easy to collect.

Unfortunately, as the pheasants begin to wake up the next morning, they start to fly up to the roof of the filling station. Mr Hazell happens to be driving past in his Rolls Royce and demands that Danny's father return them in time for his shooting party. After almost destroying his car, inside and out, the effects of the sleeping pills wear off completely and the birds fly away in the opposite direction to Mr Hazell's land and his rich guests.

There are, however, a few birds left. After giving some away, Danny and his father decide to go and inspect electric ovens – specially for roasting pheasants. Champion!

ROALD DAHL

Roald Dahl was born on 13 September 1916, in Llandaff in the Welsh capital of Cardiff. His parents were Norwegian, and the Norwegian church in Cardiff where he was baptized can still be visited in the newly redeveloped Cardiff docks. Dahl tells the sometimes painful story of his childhood and his schooling in *Boy*. In 1920 his elder sister, Astri, died of appendicitis aged seven, while two months later, his father Harald died of pneumonia. However, Roald's mother was left enough money to be able to raise the family in comfortable style. In *Boy*, Dahl portrays the casual cruelty of teachers and fellow pupils at his boarding school, Repton, in Derbyshire. But he seems to have had a fairly untroubled time there, as he was generally popular and good at games.

After leaving school at 18, Dahl joined Shell, who posted him to Dar-es-Salaam. A couple of years later, when the Second World War broke out, he immediately joined the RAF and trained as a fighter pilot. After a crash landing in which he was seriously injured, Dahl left the RAF and was posted to Washington as assistant air attaché.

It was during 1943, while in Washington, that he began to write: firstly a magazine article about his experiences in the RAF, and then a novel for children, *The Gremlins*, (originally intended to be a Disney film). He initially found success as a writer of short stories for adults, tales famous for extraordinary plots and bizarre twists. His first popular children's book was published in 1961, *James and the Giant Peach*, which grew out of a bedtime story for his children. This was followed by the best-selling *Charlie and the Chocolate Factory*. Over the next 25 years, he published a list of much-loved books including *The Magic Finger*, *Fantastic Mr Fox*, *The Twits*, *The BFG* and *Danny, The Champion of the World*. Dahl's books have been printed in 37 different languages, and their continuing success has made him the world's foremost writer for children.

Perhaps of all Dahl's books, *Danny* most clearly illustrates the Buckinghamshire world in which he lived on and off for 45 years. He bought his final home there in 1954, Gipsy House, in Great Missenden. This had a gipsy caravan in the grounds (the inspiration for the caravan in *Danny*) and also a garden shed which became Dahl's prized writing hut. He insisted that when he died, this writing hut should be left as it was during his lifetime, forever undusted.

Roald Dahl was always scrupulous in answering children's letters. He advised them that, if they wished to write, they should always make their characters extraordinary and unusual, because ordinary people were so dull. He died on 23 November 1990, and fittingly, his funeral in Great Missenden parish church was attended not only by friends and family but also by many children from the local primary school.

THE TOUR

After the Second World War, Roald Dahl lived with his mother in Buckinghamshire: firstly in Great Missenden (where the Dahl family house is now located) and then in Old Amersham. It was while in Amersham that he got to know Claud Taylor, a butcher about his own age, who taught him how to poach pheasant – a practice which, according to Dahl, was 'condoned by the right people in the countryside'.

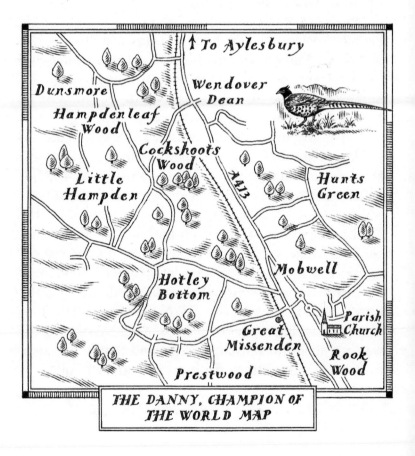

THE DANNY, CHAMPION OF
THE WORLD MAP

He first wrote about these experiences in a short story called *The Champion of the World*, which was based 12 miles from Great Missenden in the vicinity of Haddenham. The tale was later published in a collection called *Ah Sweet Mystery of Life*, before being reworked into *Danny, The Champion of the World* in 1975. In *Danny*, the location of the poaching moves to Wendover, just four miles from Great Missenden, much closer to Dahl's home and more likely to be the real location of Dahl's illicit nocturnal poaching. In the book, Danny's father mentions poaching in the area to the north of Little Hampden, near Dunsmore, and if you wander around the gently rolling Buckinghamshire hills that surround Great Missenden, you feel that you might spot Danny or his sparky father at any turn.

To visit Dahl's grave, head for the parish church at Great Missenden, where he was buried in November 1990. Walking out of the church, his grave is about 100 yards in front of you, in the large open area to the right. Next travel to Aylesbury, 10 miles from Great Missenden, to the Roald Dahl Children's Gallery. This is a must for all Dahl lovers. Housed in a remodelled 18th century coach house, complete with Great Glass Elevator, the gallery aims to bring history, natural history, science and technology to life through the world of Roald Dahl's books. For example, visitors can enter The Giant Peach, encountering insects and invertebrates with the aid of video-microscopes. Matilda's Library provides fascinating information about Roald Dahl's life and works.

THE TALES OF BEATRIX POTTER

The tales of magical Beatrix Potter characters such as Peter Rabbit and Pigling Bland have become a treasured part of our growing-up, forever linked with that first happy discovery of the pleasures of reading – or the even greater pleasure of being read to! But Beatrix Potter's own tale is every bit as fascinating as her stories. Each year, many thousands of tourists come from all over the world to visit the places in the Lake District which she wrote about and painted in her books. A visit to Beatrix Potter's house, which she gave to the National Trust, is an unforgettable experience. Stand on the back step of her old house in Sawrey and you fully expect to see Jemima Puddle-duck come waddling by or watch Samuel Whiskers scurry through a hole in the kitchen wainscot.

★ ★ ★ ★ ★

THE STORIES

The Tale of Jemima Puddle-duck
Jemima Puddle-duck is annoyed because the farmer's wife never lets her sit on her eggs. So she decides to make herself a nest in a wood, which is far away from the farm. It is here that she meets a very curious stranger indeed.

But – seated on the stump, she was startled to find an elegantly dressed gentleman reading a newspaper. He had black prick ears and sandy coloured whiskers.

Jemima agrees to make her nest in his shed, unaware that he is a fox. She is not suspicious even when he asks her to collect all the herbs used for roast duck stuffing! When her friend Kep, the collie, hears her story he goes to get help from two fox hound puppies. They manage to save Jemima, though one of the puppies rushes into the shed and gobbles up all her eggs.

The Tale of Mrs Tiggy-winkle

A kind washer-woman, Mrs Tiggy-winkle does the laundry for all the neighbouring birds and animals. She washes Cock Robin's little scarlet waistcoat and even Sally Henny-penny's yellow stockings. Looking for her lost handkerchiefs one day, a little girl called Lucie finds Mrs Tiggy-winkle's laundry upon a tiny clothes line hung up with tiny clothes pegs. Lucie is suprised to meet Mrs Tiggy-winkle with her little black nose, twinkling eyes and prickles beneath her cap,

Mrs Tiggy-winkle, illustrated by Beatrix Potter.

and is even more amazed to discover that she has washed and ironed Lucie's hankies.

There was a nice hot singey smell; and at the table, with an iron in her hand stood a very stout short person staring anxiously at Lucie.

Before she can say goodbye, Mrs T runs away. As Lucie takes another look, she sees someone very small with no apron or cap – just a hedgehog.

The Tale of Samuel Whiskers

Tabitha Twitchit is an old cat whose kittens get into all sorts of mischief. One day she cannot find Tom Kitten. He is hiding from her in what he thinks is a safe place up the chimney. But unfortunately for Tom, there are some very large, fat, old rats living in the house. Two of them, Samuel Whiskers and his wife, Anna Marie, live in a hole in the chimney.

. . .it shows how very unwise it is to go up a chimney in a very old house, where a person does not know his way, and where there are enormous rats.

When Tom bursts in on them, Samuel decides he would like some kitten dumplings and roly-poly pudding. Anna Marie quickly ties Tom up and goes to steal some dough, while Samuel gets the butter and the rolling pin. However, happily, when Samuel and Anna hear Tabitha's friend, the dog, barking, they drop the rolling pin and flee, leaving Tom rolled in dough. He never loses his fear of rats and can never chase anything bigger than a mouse!

BEATRIX POTTER

Beatrix Potter is arguably the Lake District's most successful writer, perhaps even more popular than the great poet, Wordsworth. But her life began in quite different circumstances.

Born in 1866 in Kensington, London, Beatrix led a normal life for the daughter of a wealthy family. While her younger brother Bertram was sent away to school Beatrix was taught at home, expected to bide her time until a suitable proposal of marriage came along. Encouraged by her father, Beatrix turned out to be a very able artist. She had a clear talent for sketching flowers, plants and her pets: she kept a wide assortment of animals in her nursery, ranging from rabbits and mice to bats.

The main excitement in Beatrix's life was the annual summer holiday, which lasted – not two or three weeks – but three months! Before 1882 the Potters used to go every year to Perthshire in Scotland. However when Beatrix was 16 they changed their destination. For the next 21 years the Potters took their annual holiday in the Lake District, always with Beatrix accompanying them.

As Beatrix grew older, no marriage proposal was forthcoming. She continued to keep her pets, and two rabbits were particular favourites: Benjamin Bunny and Peter Piper (also known as Peter Rabbit). Some designs featuring Benjamin Bunny for a greetings card were accepted by a firm which paid her £6.

Encouraged by Canon Rawnsley, a Lake District friend, Beatrix next wrote a story called *The Tale of Peter Rabbit and Mr McGregor's Garden*. Unable to find a publisher, she had the book printed herself. Later the publishers, Frederick Warne and Sons, agreed to publish the book: it came out on 2 October 1902 and was an immediate success. By the end of 1903, 50,000 copies of the book had been printed.

In 1905, Beatrix Potter, now with money of her own, bought Hill Top farm in Sawrey. 'It is as nearly perfect a little place as I ever lived in, and such nice old-fashioned people in the village,' she wrote. The house became a rich source of inspiration for her work. Out of the 13 books she wrote after 1905, six are set in Hill Top and Sawrey, including the tales of Samuel Whiskers and Jemima Puddle-duck. Beatrix Potter continued to spend much of her money buying Lake District farms and land. Her father had been a founder member of the National Trust, set up in 1895 to preserve places of natural beauty.

In 1913, aged 47, Beatrix Potter married William Heelis, a Hawkshead solicitor who handled her growing list of Lakeland property transactions. Once married, she more or less gave up writing to concentrate on farming and acquiring more land to be preserved in the traditional Lakeland way. She became an expert on Herdwick sheep, the native sheep of the Lake District.

Beatrix Potter continued her quiet Lakeland life until she died on 22 December 1943 with her husband at her side. She left her 4,000 acres of land, 14 farms and various cottages to the National Trust. Her book sales now total several million, with most sold in America and a growing number in Japan. And, interestingly, the majority of visitors to the places on the Beatrix Potter trail are grown-ups!

THE TOUR

Beatrix Potter and her writings have stimulated quite a substantial tourist business in the Lake District, with no fewer than four separate Beatrix Potter attractions.

The first one to head for is in the picturesque village of Near Sawrey, which provided the settings for several of her animal tales. (Look out for the Tower Bank Arms which appears in *Jemima Puddle-duck* and Buckle Yeat, now a guest house and teashop, which appears as the Duchess's house in *The Pie and The Patty-Pan*.) Here you will find Beatrix Potter's former home, Hill Top. Now owned by the National Trust, it would be a delightful place to visit even without its famous literary connections. Lovers of the Potter books will find Hill Top instantly recognisable. Walk up the path to the house, for example, and you will see that this was the path up which Tom, Mittens and Moppet were led in disgrace by Mrs Tabitha Twitchit in *The Tale of Tom Kitten*. And near the house is the green metal gate where Jemima Puddle-duck makes her decision to fly away. Look carefully and you

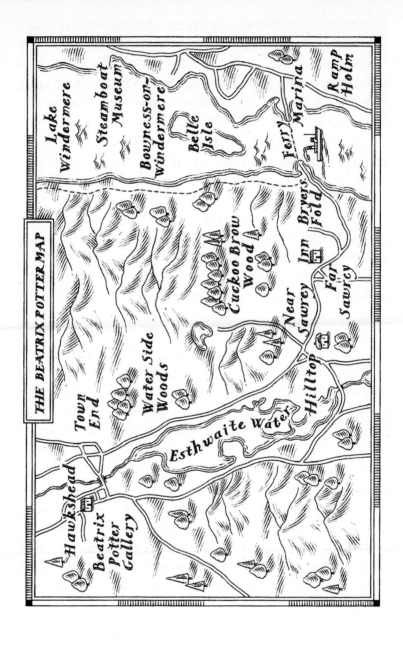

THE BEATRIX POTTER MAP

might spot a watering can on the wall, similar to the one in which Peter Rabbit hides from Mr McGregor.

The inside of the fine old 17th century house is just as familiar. In the kitchen is the magnificent old dresser which was used as a backdrop in *The Tailor of Gloucester* and *The Tale of Samuel Whiskers,* and you will see that the old range is the one up which Tom Kitten put his head. Up the stairs is the very landing where Mrs Tabitha Twitchit stood and 'mewed dreadfully' for her son, Thomas. And at the back of the house is the New Room where between 1905 and 1913 Beatrix Potter produced seven of her best-loved books. From the window in this room you can see Stoney Lane as it was drawn in *The Tale of Samuel Whiskers*.

From Hill Top, you should travel to Hawkshead, the town in *The Tale of Johnny Town-mouse.* Here in the Beatrix Potter Gallery, housed in the former offices of her husband, the solicitor William Heelis, you can see a delightful selection of Beatrix Potter's original drawings and illustrations.

In Bowness-on-Windermere there is a year-round 'World of Beatrix Potter' Exhibition where her famous animal characters are brought to life. You can see Peter Rabbit in his radish patch, Mrs Tiggy-winkle in her cave and Jeremy Fisher the frog in his pond. Tea can be taken with Simpkin the cat in The Tailor of Gloucester Tea Room.

Finally, in Keswick, visit Beatrix Potter's Lake District Exhibition. This multi-media show explains the author's important conservation work in the area.

FURTHER INFORMATION

Hill Top, owned by the National Trust, is in the village of Near
Sawrey, reached by ferry across Lake Windermere from Bowness.
It is closed during the winter.
The Beatrix Potter Gallery in Hawkshead, also owned by the
National Trust, is closed during the winter.
The World of Beatrix Potter Exhibition in Bowness-on-Windermere
is open all year round.
Beatrix Potter's Lake District in Keswick is open from
Easter to Christmas.

CARRIE'S WAR
by Nina Bawden

The momentous period of the Second World War turned the lives of city children upside down. Many of them had never been away from home before, let alone unaccompanied by their parents. Now they were suddenly uprooted and sent to unknown, but safer, areas in the countryside in order to protect them from the much-feared German bombing. For many it was a very distressing experience.

In the years after the War, many excellent books appeared which offered a child's point of view of those extraordinary times. Some are highly dramatic (such as Robert Westall's *The Machine Gunners*, for example), others are funny (read the highly-amusing *William* stories by Richmal Crompton). *Carrie's War* describes a wartime experience which clearly did much to shape the author's later life. Nina Bawden was 14 years old and living, fairly comfortably, in London when the War started. Her period of evacuation taught her about life in a different world, a Welsh mining valley. But, just as importantly, she learnt perhaps even more about herself.

THE STORY

The story begins with the adult Carrie revisiting the small town where she and her younger brother Nick were evacuated during the Second World War. But showing her children her old home doesn't bring back any happy memories.

Places change more than people, perhaps. You don't change, you know, growing older. I thought I had changed, that I'd feel differently now . . . I did a dreadful thing, the worst thing of my life, when I was twelve and a half years old, or I feel that I did, and nothing can change it . . .

Thirty years earlier, Carrie and Nick leave London on a train, labelled like parcels. They arrive in Wales and are taken in by kindly Auntie Lou and her bad-tempered brother Mr Evans. However, on settling into their new home they soon adapt to Mr Evans's tyrannical nature.

Mr Evans has an older sister, Dilys, who many years ago had married an English mine owner, Mr Gotobed. Mr Evans blamed him for the death of his father in a pit accident and he had never let bygones be bygones. Mrs Gotobed is now an old lady, looked after by the kindly Hepzibah Green. Hepzibah has also taken Mr Johnny Gotobed, a distant cousin, under her wing. They all live in Druid's Bottom, formerly a very grand house in Druid's Grove surrounded by dark yew trees. The children's first visit there is very spooky. Hepzibah tells them the tale of the screaming skull, which will bring disaster if it is removed from the house. Carrie's vivid imagination works overtime, but the warmth of Hepzibah's kitchen soothes her. The kitchen becomes a sanctuary for the children.

Hepzibah's kitchen was always like that . . . Coming into it was like coming home on a bitter cold day to a bright, leaping fire. It was like the smell of bacon when you were hungry; loving arms when you were lonely; safety when you were scared . . .

It later appears that Mr Evans is very jealous of Hepzibah, feeling that Druid's Bottom really ought to be his after his sister dies. One day, Mrs Gotobed gives Carrie a message for Mr Evans, which is to be passed on after her death. She says she hasn't forgotten that her brother is her flesh and blood, but that sometimes we owe more to strangers. When the time comes and Carrie passes this message on, Mr Evans explodes with rage against Hepzibah, saying that as his sister left no will, Hepzibah and Mr Johnny are to leave Druid's Bottom within a month. Mr Evans has been to the house and looked through his sister's things, and we're made to wonder if he, in fact, took a homemade will which Mrs Gotobed kept in her jewel box. Carrie cannot believe it. She knows Mr Evans is mean, but never thinks he is dishonest.

Out of the blue, Carrie and Nick receive a letter from their mother asking them to join her in Glasgow. Carrie feels torn in two, and Mr Evans softens towards the children, giving Nick a knife and Carrie a beautiful gold and garnet ring. The children have a last tea at Druid's Bottom with Hepzibah and Carrie shows off the ring. It looks very much like one of Mrs Gotobed's – did Mr Evans steal it, along with the will? The angry Carrie secretly takes the screaming skull and throws it into the horse pond in order to bring the curse down on Druid's Bottom so Mr Evans can't enjoy what is rightfully Hepzibah's. However, her sympathies change towards him when she finds out that Mr Evans is in fact as honest as she always thought him to be.

As the train to Glasgow rushes by, the children take one last look at Druid's Bottom. Carrie screams. The house is ablaze! Was it the curse of the skull? Is it all Carrie's fault? 30 years later she still feels guilty, but thankfully her children piece the story together for her and discover a happy ending.

★　　★　　★　　★　　★

NINA BAWDEN

In her autobiography, Nina Bawden explains that 'Carrie's war' is not quite the same as 'Nina's war'. Although her story is essentially a work of fiction, there are many similarities between her real-life experiences and those recounted by Carrie in the book.

Born in 1925, Nina Bawden was evacuated with her school, first to Ipswich in Suffolk, then to Aberdare in South Wales. Although sad to leave her family, Nina enjoyed her period of evacuation, always finding life in other people's homes interesting. It was not always as expected, however. Nina recalls how one girl was so shocked by finding that the only lavatory was at the bottom of a cottage garden that she went back to London at the end of the first week. Most of all, Nina enjoyed the new freedom she discovered as an evacuee, as most adults didn't have much time for them.

Almost all of the families that Nina stayed with had characteristics which she 'borrowed' when creating the fictional Samuel Isaac Evans, his sister Lou and their Welsh grocery shop, 30 years later. There was the house-proud woman who refused to allow Nina to go upstairs more than twice a day, in case her feet wore out the stair carpet. And there was her short stay in a chemist's shop, where Nina helped behind the counter, occasionally being allowed to count saccharines into packets of a hundred.

After graduating from Oxford University, Nina Bawden became a full-time writer. She has written more than 20 adult books and many successful children's books including *The Secret Passage* and *The Peppermint Pig* in addition to the most successful, *Carrie's War*, published in 1973.

★　★　★　★　★

THE TOUR

When the television rights for *Carrie's War* were bought by the BBC in 1976, Nina Bawden was astonished to discover that without any guidance from her, the director intended to shoot the film in the town of Blaengarw, about 30 minutes' drive from Cardiff. It was here that Nina had arrived by train in the spring of 1940, misdirected when her rail carriage was separated from the part of the train carrying all her schoolfriends to their correct destination in Aberdare. However, until the mistake was rectified, Nina spent a happy week in Blaengarw with a hospitable mining family. It wasn't until she returned to the town 30 years later to watch the filming that she realised how much the fictional town in *Carrie's War* had been influenced by that first experience of Blaengarw in 1940. That first sight of a mining valley with its huge slag heaps and pit machinery had never really been erased from her mind.

Now, Blaengarw's mine is long gone and the town is facing very hard times. But visiting it today you can still imagine the place that Carrie discovered when she arrived at the station. The town still boasts several grand chapels and a fine workman's hall, a characteristic feature of the mining valleys in Wales. According to a handsome, colourful mosaic which decorates the outside wall, it cost £3400 when it was built in 1897 from funds deducted from miners' wages. Because of the appalling hard work and danger of labouring underground, the men were fiercely proud of the cultural life provided by the 'institute' – the male voice choirs and the well-appointed reading room.

Just along the street from the workman's hall is the sort of grocery where Carrie and her brother might have lived with Samuel Isaac Evans and his meek sister Lou. Behind the modern changes (it is now a self-

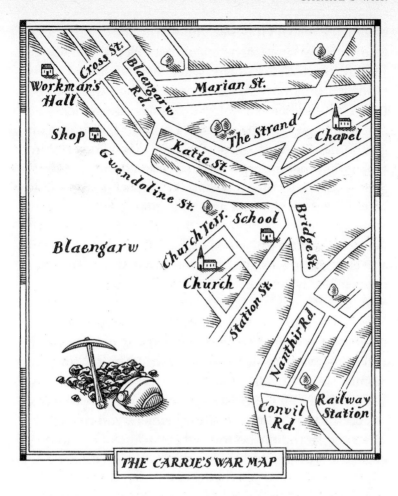

THE CARRIE'S WAR MAP

service supermarket, the '8am till 8pm'), it is possible
to detect the vestiges of a handsomely-fitted store.
Standing in the shop, you can easily imagine Carrie
and her brother here all those years ago.

But where is Druid's Bottom? You can scour the
outskirts of Blaengarw (on a sunny day there are some
fine walks up the valley), but you will not find this

81

imaginary place. However, the warm and comfortable farm house where Carrie encounters Hepzibah, Mister Johnny, and Mr Evans's sister Mrs Gotobed, was modelled on an actual farmhouse, though this is to be found in another part of the country altogether. The place Nina Bawden had in mind was the farmhouse on the border between Shropshire and Montgomeryshire that her mother moved to from London during the Blitz. She fondly remembers a happy summer spent there, helping with the harvest and collecting eggs.

To actually experience today what life used to be like in a Welsh mining village, and feel what Carrie and her brother felt when they stepped off that wartime train, visit the Rhondda Heritage Park at the Old Lewis Merthyr Colliery, near Pontypridd. The Visitor Centre exhibition contains an indoor village street, complete with shop frontages and interiors, where you can imagine Samuel Isaac Evans and his sister doing business. Visitors here can even discover what it was like to work underground. Putting on safety helmets, you ride down in a cage to the pit bottom where you explore underground roadways and the workings of the colliery.

FURTHER INFORMATION

The Rhondda Heritage Park is open daily with tours at regular intervals throughout the day. It is closed on Mondays from October to Easter.

THE WIND IN THE WILLOWS

by *Kenneth Grahame*

First published in 1908, *The Wind in the Willows* is one of those classic books that almost immediately became a part of British life. But the delightfully crafted tale of Mole, Rat, Badger and the excellent Mr Toad was initially rejected by many publishers. Even when the novel finally emerged, the critics didn't quite know how to take it. For instance, one reviewer for *The Times* thought it was a very unsatisfactory work about the life of river bank animals!

Ever since its slow start the book has sold extremely well, and its success has been followed by numerous adaptations. In 1930 a stage version was first performed, *Toad of Toad Hall* by A A Milne, author of *Winnie the Pooh*. (E H Shepard, who illustrated *Pooh*, also later provided the best-loved illustrations for *The Wind in the Willows*.) The story has been made into various TV and film productions, as well as being adapted into a theatre play by Alan Bennett.

Kenneth Grahame lived near, and loved, the River Thames all his life. His story offers a double pleasure, as many of the locations described in the book can be visited in one memorable outing.

THE STORY

Tired of spring-cleaning his little underground home, Mole flings his brush to the floor and scrapes and scrabbles his way to daylight. Something up above is calling him. He happily scrambles through the meadows until he reaches the river, which he has never before encountered. Here he meets Rat, who has his home on the river bank, and immediately they become firm friends. In the days and weeks that follow, the good-natured Rat teaches Mole rowing and swimming, and they spend many summer afternoons having idyllic riverside picnics and simply 'messing about in boats'.

Rat soon introduces Mole to the jolly good-humoured Toad, who is famous for his fads, squandering his rather large fortune on impossible dreams. He begs Rat and Mole to join him for a few days enjoying his newest craze – a gipsy caravan. However, while out on the open road, a motor-car flies past which wrecks the caravan, frightens the horse and makes the caged bird sob.

Toad, by E H Shepard.

Undaunted, the next morning Toad goes into town and orders an expensive new motor-car.

*All those wasted years that lie behind me, I never
knew, never even dreamt! . . . What dust-clouds shall
spring up behind me as I speed on my reckless way!
What carts shall I fling carelessly into the ditch in the
wake of my magnificent onset! Horrid little carts –
common carts – canary-coloured carts!*

Mole has a terrifying adventure when he sets off to
the Wild Wood to find Badger but becomes lost.
Luckily Rat finds him, and, on coming across Badger's
front door by chance, they spend a comfortable night
after all.

One day Rat and Mole are returning from a hunting
expedition with Otter, when Mole catches the scent of
his old home and is strongly pulled towards it. They
are rushing around lighting fires and dusting when
carol-singing field mice arrive.

*In the forecourt, lit by the dim rays of a horn
lantern, some eight or ten little field-mice stood in a
semi-circle, red worsted comforters round their
throats, their fore-paws thrust deep into their
pockets, their feet jigging for warmth.*

Rat sends out for food and they all have a feast. But
although Mole enjoys being home, he knows he must
return to the river bank.

Badger visits to tell Rat and Mole that the time has
come to teach the careless Toad some sense. They
attempt to keep him prisoner in Toad Hall while he
learns the error of his ways, but although appearing

sorry, Toad refuses to give up cars. He escapes out of a window and dances away along the road. Stopping for lunch at an inn, he unfortunately gives in to temptation and steals a motor-car which halts outside. He is hauled up in front of a magistrate and is sentenced to 20 years' imprisonment in the grimmest dungeon.

The gaoler's daughter takes pity on Toad and helps him to escape, disguised as a washer-woman. So begin his adventures to get home. He manages to hitch a ride first on a train and then on a barge. Both end badly and he is no nearer Toad Hall, yet he becomes puffed up with conceit because he has not been caught.

Ho, ho, I am The Toad, the handsome, the popular, the successful Toad!

He decides he wants to arrive home in style and hails a passing motor-car – the very motor-car which he stole from the inn. Fortunately he is not recognised but, realising this, he becomes more courageous, asks to drive, and finally loses his head by telling the occupants that he is the 'entirely fearless Toad'. They try to seize him and Toad crashes the car into a horse pond. He escapes, falls into the river, and luckily comes upon Rat's hole.

Rat breaks the news that Toad Hall has been taken over by Wild Wooders, though Mole and Badger are doing their best to keep an eye on it. Eventually the four friends, armed with cudgels, bravely reclaim Toad's ancestral home. At a celebratory banquet, an altered Toad refuses to make speeches or to take any credit. However, the adventures at Toad Hall live on afterwards among the river bank dwellers.

Rat and Mole,
illustrated by E H Shepard.

KENNETH GRAHAME

Born in 1859, the third child in a prosperous Edinburgh family, Kenneth Grahame spent his early years idyllically near Loch Fyne. However, when he was nearly five his mother died of scarlet fever. Unable to cope with the children, his father sent them to live with their grandmother in Cookham Dean, a village near the River Thames. Young Kenneth Grahame fell in love with the river and spent much of his boyhood exploring its secret places, discovering the pleasures of 'simply messing about in boats'.

After attending school in Oxford, there was not enough money for Grahame to continue his studies at Oxford University. Instead, he took a job as a clerk at the Bank of England. Grahame quickly rose through the ranks, finally becoming the youngest Secretary of the Bank of England at the age of just 39. Despite this demanding job, Grahame found plenty of time to indulge his passion for writing and travelling. His first book *Pagan Papers* was published in 1893, followed by two books about childhood, *The Golden Age* in 1895 and *Dream Days* in 1898.

Kenneth Grahame married Elspeth Thomson in July 1899 and the following year they had a son, Alastair, known to them as Mouse. It was Grahame's bedtime stories to Mouse, begun in 1904, that eventually became *The Wind in the Willows*. Shortly before its publication Grahame retired from the Bank, though afterwards, he wrote very little.

After returning to lease a house in Cookham Dean, the Grahames moved to Blewbury on the northern edge of the Berkshire Downs. Following the death of Mouse at the age of just 20, the Grahames moved to a house in Pangbourne on Kenneth's beloved Thames. It was here at Church Cottage that Kenneth Grahame died on 6 July 1932. His funeral was held at the adjacent church, St James the Less.

Grahame's body was later moved to Holywell Cemetery, Oxford, to lie beside Mouse. The epitaph on his headstone, written by novelist Anthony Hope, reads:

*To the beautiful memory of Kenneth Grahame . . .
who passed the River on the 6th July 1932, leaving
childhood and literature through him the more blest
for all time.*

THE TOUR

Begin the tour in the Berkshire village where Kenneth Grahame first came to know the Thames, Cookham Dean. He lived here with his grandmother in a 300-year-old hunting lodge called The Mount; a great tree in the extensive grounds marked the former edge of Windsor Forest. The years that Grahame spent here were among the happiest in his life.

Lying between Cookham Dean and the Thames is Grahame's model for the Wild Wood, Quarry Wood, which still remains pleasingly wild. At its entrance, a Woodland Trust sign lists the rich variety of plants and birds to be found here.

Grahame's inspiration for Toad Hall came from several grand homes near the Thames. It was partly inspired by the imposing mansion of Cliveden, which stands high on a hill above Cookham. Cliveden is now an expensive hotel but the grounds are National Trust property and can still be visited. Another inspirational property was Harleyford Manor. This lies a few miles upstream from Marlow and is now a golf course – one feels that Toad might have rather approved of golf! However, the principal model for

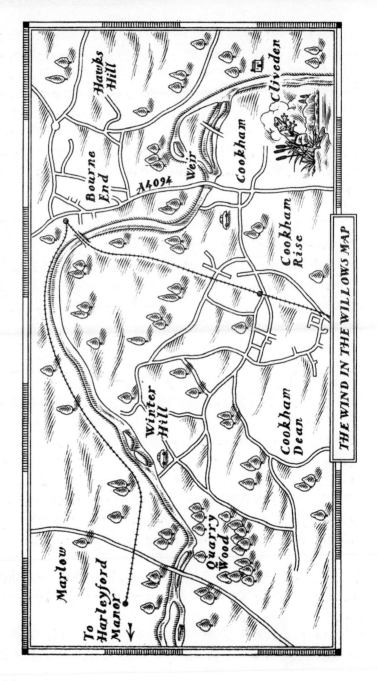

Toad Hall is Mapledurham House, which lies on the north bank of the Thames a few miles upstream from Reading. This stately home, open to the public from Easter to the end of September, is the one used by E H Shepard in his famous illustration of Toad Hall. And it looks every inch a residence suitable for Mr Toad, with original moulded ceilings and a great oak staircase. It's easy to imagine Toad escaping from his bedroom on knotted sheets!

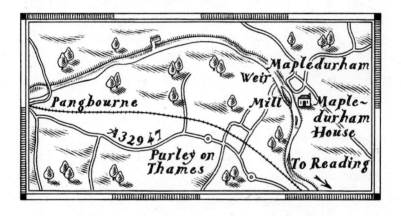

The grim gaol to which Toad is committed is most certainly Reading Gaol (in which the writer Oscar Wilde had been famously imprisoned). The old Gaol has been demolished, but the new Gaol, which can be seen in the centre of Reading not far from the railway station, looks quite as terrifying as its predecessor.

It is no surprise that Grahame chose to live out the final years of his life in Pangbourne. Here the Thames still evokes Grahame's long-ago descriptions of river life. And his final home, Church Cottage, still looks much as it did when Grahame lived there. At the end of the garden you can still see the round village lock-up which the writer used as his tool shed!

For a real *Wind in the Willows* treat, on a warm sunny day, take a picnic and hire a rowing boat from Pangbourne. When you tie up on the river bank, look about carefully and you may find that from the shadows you are being watched by a mole, a rat, a badger – or even a toad!

TOM BROWN'S SCHOOLDAYS
by Thomas Hughes

T *om Brown's Schooldays* reveals some of the horrors of life in a public school towards the beginning of Queen Victoria's reign. Rugby School is today considered one of the finest of England's public schools and the birthplace of one of the world's most popular sports. But in the 1820s, much like other schools of its sort in those times, it was a rough, brutal place where teaching was often abysmal and bullying was rife. *Tom Brown's Schooldays* was the first book to describe all of this in unflinching detail. However, it also shows how this public school was civilised by its idealistic, inspirational headmaster, Dr Arnold. The extraordinary success of the book, published in 1857, helped to establish Rugby School's place in national life, with many thousands of school boys taking the book's ideals with them when they later went out into the world.

One of the great pleasures of *Tom Brown's Schooldays* is that it not only recreates the day-to-day world of a public school, but also other aspects of ordinary life in 1830s England. Tom Brown's stage-coach journey from his Berkshire home to Rugby is a delightful, beautifully-written account. 'The music of the rattling harness, and the ring of the horses' feet on the hard road, and the glare of the two bright lamps through the steaming hoar frost . . .' makes you feel as if you are right there, riding with Tom, as the coach races through the dark English countryside.

The novel is semi-autobiographical, and for anyone who wants to travel in the footsteps of Tom Brown, Rugby School remains largely as Thomas Hughes described it. Not only can you see the Close where Tom Brown had his first taste of rugby football, you can still touch the graffitied desk lids, wood panelling, stone walls and columns into which thousands of Tom Browns have been diligently carving their names for more than 200 years.

★   ★   ★   ★   ★

THE STORY

Tom Brown doesn't actually begin his schooldays until almost a quarter of the way into the book. We are first introduced to our young hero in his home in the Vale of the White Horse.

And then what a hill is the White Horse Hill! There it stands right up above all the rest, nine hundred feet above the sea, and the boldest, bravest shape for a chalk hill that you ever saw.

A picture of rural bliss and youthful contentment is painted, though Tom is keen to give this up for the unknown hazards of Rugby School.

A Rugby pupil, by Sidney Hall.

Arriving in Rugby, Tom is quickly taken under the wing of another pupil, Harry 'Scud' East, who introduces him to the school and its customs. Tom immediately takes part in his first rugby football match and distinguishes himself by saving a try. He also soon hears his first sermon delivered by headmaster Dr Arnold, who encourages the pupils to 'strive against whatever was mean and unmanly and unrighteous in our little world'.

Not long afterwards, Tom suffers unrighteously at the hands of the bully Flashman. He is roasted at the open fire in School-house Hall when he refuses to give up his lottery ticket.

'. . . let's roast him,' cried Flashman, and catches hold of Tom by the collar: one or two boys hesitate, but the rest join in. East seizes Tom's arm and tries to pull him away, but is knocked back by one of the boys, and Tom is dragged along struggling. His shoulders are pushed against the mantelpiece, and he is held by main force before the fire, Flashman drawing his trousers tight by way of extra torture.

Tom and 'Scud' East decide to confront Flashman and, though both smaller than him, take him on in a fight. Like most other bullies, Flashman proves to be a coward. When he falls and bangs his head, he admits defeat. Flashman 'never laid a finger on either of them again' and is later expelled for drunkenness.

Tom and East then get into a series of minor scrapes. Their misdemeanours include inscribing their names on the minute-hand of the great clock. In doing so, they slow the clock down, making half of the school late for prayers the next morning.

The following term, Tom is made to share a study with George Arthur, a shy bookish boy who becomes an object of derision on his first night in the dormitory when he kneels at the foot of his bed to say his prayers. Tom looks after Arthur (he begins to say his prayers like him to spare him further derision) and Arthur's influence has a beneficial effect on Tom. At the end of the book we discover that this is exactly what Dr Arnold had hoped.

Tom's protection of Arthur gets him involved in a bruising fist-fight with 'Slogger' Williams, which ends – with honours – after the arrival of Dr Arnold. Tom's final success at Rugby is to captain the school cricket team in a match against an MCC (Marylebone Cricket Club) side.

The story ends in 1842, when Tom hears by chance of the death of Dr Arnold. He immediately travels back to Rugby to stand at the grave of his old headmaster

THOMAS HUGHES

Some of the facts of the author's life are sketched at the start of *Tom Brown's Schooldays*. Born in 1822 at Uffington (a small Berkshire village in the Vale of the White Horse), Thomas Hughes was the son of a country gentleman. In the book, he writes with affection of life in a countryside which was soon to be altered forever by the Industrial Revolution and the coming of the railway. (Brunel's epoch-making Great Western Railway passed very near to Uffington.)

In 1834, Thomas Hughes was sent to Rugby with his brother, George. Dr Arnold had been in charge of the school for five years by the time he arrived. Thomas was not academically gifted, never becoming one of Dr Arnold's special pupils, but he did become captain of football and cricket teams. In 1842, the year that Dr Arnold died, Hughes left Rugby for Oriel College, Oxford, where he obtained his degree in 1845.

Rugby School, illustrated by Sidney Hall.

Hughes then went to London to train as a barrister. His privileged upbringing provided no preparation for the shocking scenes of poverty and hardship he encountered here – the life of London's poor which was so graphically described by Charles Dickens. As a result, and because Dr Arnold had encouraged support for the underdog, Hughes became involved in politics. He campaigned for Chartism, supporting the causes of trade unions and workers' groups, and arguing that everyone, not just the wealthy, should be entitled to vote.

In 1847, Thomas Hughes married Frances Ford, a clergyman's daughter he'd met at Oxford. He continued to practise as a barrister for the next 10 years until writing *Tom Brown's Schooldays* in 1856, at the age of 34. He began the book as something for his eight-year-old son to read before his own arrival at public school. When published the following year, it was immediately successful, selling out five editions in just seven months. While Hughes did write other books, including a sequel, *Tom Brown at Oxford*, nothing came close to matching the success of his first work.

He continued to be involved in politics and was elected in 1865 as MP for Lambeth and in 1868 as MP for Frome, though his political career was not judged a success. In 1879 Hughes put his money into a scheme to establish a colony (called Rugby) for public schoolboys in the American state of Tennessee – even boasting an Arnold School. But this too proved to be an unhappy failure. He finally moved to Chester and became a County Court judge in 1882.

Hughes died at the age of 73 in Brighton, whilst on his way to Italy. The fortune he had earned from the sales of *Tom Brown's Schooldays* – which had run to over 70 editions in his lifetime – had all been generously spent on a succession of philanthropic schemes. In his will he left just £8000. But with *Tom Brown's Schooldays*, many would say he bequeathed a priceless legacy.

★　　★　　★　　★　　★

THE TOUR

It is a sign of Rugby School's special place in English life that it offers year-round guided tours. And tours led, not by a professional guide, but by a pupil of the school – a real-life Tom Brown (or Tammy Brown, as the school is now co-educational!).

The visit starts at the excellent Rugby School Museum, which in a series of thoughtful displays tells the history of the school from its foundation in 1567. As well as information about the life of Thomas Hughes and exhibits relating to *Tom Brown's Schooldays* (including the hands of the clock which Tom inscribed), the museum has information about other famous 'old boys', such as the poet Rupert Brooke (who was born in Rugby), Lewis Carroll and Arthur Ransome. Upstairs there a fascinating display about the life and work of Dr Arnold: look out for the painstakingly handwritten play penned by Arnold when he was a boy.

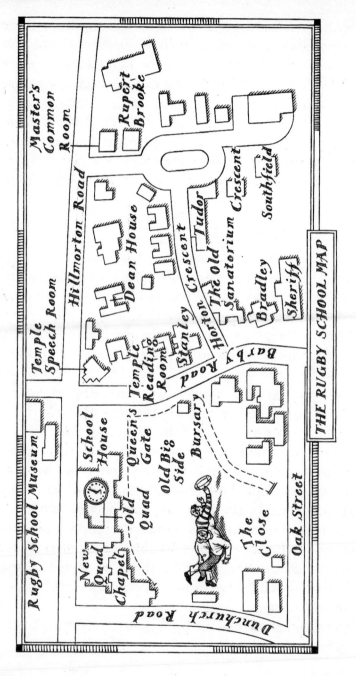

THE RUGBY SCHOOL MAP

From the museum, an absorbing behind-the-scenes walk takes you through many of the recognisable settings from *Tom Brown's Schooldays*. First, you have a chance to meet Thomas Hughes himself – or at least the statue of him which stands beside the school tuck shop. Across the road from the statue is the Close, where Tom played football on his first day. On the wall at the north end of the Close is a plaque which records the legendary exploits of William Webb Ellis.

Nearby is the Island. This was the scene of the infamous School Rebellion in 1797, when the boys had a violent disagreement with their headmaster and blew his study door off its hinges with a bomb. The headmaster responded with mass floggings, while the boys replied by smashing every window in the school. After making a bonfire of desks in the Close, the boys took refuge on the Island (which was surrounded by a moat and spanned by a drawbridge), until it was eventually besieged by a small party of militia assisted by local farmers armed with horse whips.

Moving on to the School-house, notice the turret built by Dr Arnold to provide boys with direct access to his study. Tom's much-loved headmaster is buried in the school chapel, beneath the pulpit from which he delivered his famous sermons. Baron de Coubertin read *Tom Brown's Schooldays* and so admired what it told him of sport at Rugby that he travelled from France to visit the school. He later said that it was while gazing upon Dr Arnold's grave that he was inspired with the idea of inaugurating the Modern Olympic games.

The buildings around the Old Quad seem to have barely changed in 150 years. It would not be surprising to spot Tom Brown and 'Scud' East stepping out of a classroom door. The most striking sight is the names of boys carved into almost every wooden panel or stone wall. In Upper Bench, where Dr Arnold did most of his teaching, you can even see the name of former British Prime Minister and Rugby old boy, Neville Chamberlain, carved into a desk lid. In the Old Big Schoolroom, look for the carefully carved horses in the wood panelling.

Outside, in the quad itself, you can see the old water pump, under which Tom was ducked. And up above the quad is the school clock, where Tom and East climbed to carve their names into the clock's minute-hand.

FURTHER INFORMATION

You will find Rugby School Museum at 10 Little Church Street, Rugby CV21 3AW. Contact the Museum to check opening times before you visit.

THE SHEEP-PIG
by Dick King-Smith

The story of a pig who literally saves his bacon by becoming a sheep-dog would seem to be a very unlikely plot for a major Hollywood hit movie, but the film *Babe*, based on Dick King-Smith's book *The Sheep-Pig*, has been one of the most successful films of the 1990s. It captured the imagination of the world. At the peak of the film's popularity in America, sales of bacon, sausages and pork were said to have dropped by 20 per cent while, afraid of the effect the film might have in Ireland, Irish farmers tried to have *Babe* banned!

However, the story behind the tale of how one pig and his impossible dream reached the silver screen is even more fascinating. It begins in a field in a Bristol suburb, before taking in the countryside of New South Wales in Australia, en route to the Hollywood studios of Los Angeles. And at its centre is a man who started his working life as a farmer, who later became a teacher, and who is finally acclaimed as one of the world's best-selling children's authors.

THE STORY

At the village fair, Farmer Hogget's attention is drawn to a squealing noise which is coming from a small pen. Inside is a piglet: for 10 pence, people are offered the chance to win him by guessing his weight. Farmer Hogget has a try and, to his surprise, he wins the pig.

Back at Farmer Hogget's farm, the piglet is very homesick. 'I want my mum,' he tells Fly, the sheep-dog, who decides to look after him. She discovers that the piglet's mother called him and all his brothers and sisters the same name – Babe.

When Fly trains her puppies to be sheep-dogs Babe joins in and soon asks, 'Why can't I learn to be a sheep-pig?'. But the dogs control the sheep by cunning and intimidation, while Babe learns his success from an old lame ewe called Ma. She tells him that she hates 'wolves' (the word she uses for the sheep-dogs) and that if someone were as polite to her as Babe, she'd do anything they asked.

While Farmer Hogget and Fly are out at market one day, Babe decides to go and do some rounding up of the sheep. As he gets to the top of the hill which over-looks the sheep field, he sees a strange cattle lorry with two men and their dogs herding the flock towards it. Babe manages to foil the rustlers by politely asking the sheep to stop. But the dogs and the men turn on Babe, who squeals loudly enough to alert Mrs Hogget, who in turn calls the police. As a reward for his bravery,

Babe escapes the butcher's knife and is kept as a pet. From then on, Babe is very popular with the sheep.

> '*We want Babe!*' they bleated.

Farmer Hogget develops a suspicion that Babe, who works as well as any trained dog, is a very good 'sheep-pig', and enters him for the Grand Challenge Sheep-Dog Trials. When Babe enters the course with Farmer Hogget the crowd gasps and laughs. But this soon turns to cheers as Babe is awarded 100 out of 100 – a perfect score. Farmer Hogget bends down and scratches Babe between the ears:

> '*That'll do,*' said Farmer Hogget to his sheep-pig. '*That'll do.*'

★　　★　　★　　★　　★

DICK KING-SMITH

Born in Gloucestershire in 1923, the son of a paper mill owner, Dick King-Smith went to Marlborough School as a boarder. He enjoyed his time there, though it was a strange time to be at school. Just before Dick King-Smith left Marlborough, the Second World War began and many of his friends were killed.

At the age of 21 Dick married Myrle, a girl he had known since he was 13. But a year afterwards Dick was called up to join the army, finding himself fighting the retreating Germans in Italy with the Grenadier Guards. In July 1944 he was nearly killed when a grenade thrown by a German paratrooper exploded near him and pieces of metal pierced his lung. Three years later, after leaving the army and recovering from his injuries, Dick took on a 50-acre pig farm at Coalpit Heath, near Bristol, which he ran with his wife for 14 years. His favourite pig, a large white called Monty (who he kept from 1950 to 1958), was the pig who provided the inspiration for *Babe*. Monty is the star of the 1993 book *All Pigs Are Beautiful*. It contains an illustration in which Dick King-Smith is scratching the head of the huge Monty, who weighed 600 lbs (over 42 stone!) and who had a voracious appetite – particularly for eating mud!

He left Coalpit Heath to take on the tenancy of a bigger 200-acre farm at Siston, also near Bristol, where he had a large dairy herd. But unfortunately, he was not a successful farmer, due to his lack of expertise in business. After the bank manager 'pulled the plug' on the farm Dick found himself, at the age of 45, with three children and no job. After trying, unsuccessfully, to sell fire-fighting suits, then working as an engineer at a shoe factory, he decided he had to find a new career.

Dick's daughter was about to begin teacher training and she suggested that he should do the same. He obtained a degree in education at the age of 53 and began teaching at a local primary school. However, in his spare time, he also began to write, and after seven years he had produced four books. Aged 60, he decided to give up teaching for good and to concentrate full-time on writing.

After retiring from school, Dick says the books 'sprang up like mushrooms'. From his very first published book, *The Fox Busters*, it was clear he had a rare talent. At a rate of about eight books a year, he has now written more than 80, including *Harry's Mad* and *The Queen's Nose*, both of which have been filmed for television. The latter story, and his series about a six-year-old farm girl called Sophie, are inspired by his wife, Myrle. Of all his books, Dick King-Smith is sure which one is his favourite: *The Sheep-Pig*. He was also very pleased with the film version. But the success of *Babe* has brought the problem of a bulging postbag. Dick has always tried to provide a personal answer to the many letters he receives from readers every week. He has now had to employ an assistant to help with all the correspondence.

THE TOUR

The film rights to *The Sheep-Pig* were bought by an Australian producer, and *Babe* was filmed near the small Australian town of Robertson in the Southern Highlands of New South Wales, an area south-west of Sydney. However, the story was actually set on Dick King-Smith's first farm at Coalpit Heath, near Bristol.

Woodlands Farm, where the King-Smiths lived for 14 years is a charming place. As it is on private land, it is not open to the public. But you can glimpse the original home of *Babe* from a nearby public footpath.

To reach the farm you will need to travel by car. Leave the M4 at Junction 19, which takes you on to the M32. Leave the M32 immediately at Junction 1 and follow the A4174 Ring Road eastwards. At the second roundabout, head north up the Badminton Road towards Coalpit Heath. Woodlands Farm lies on the left, immediately after passing beneath the high railway viaduct. The footpath which passes the farm

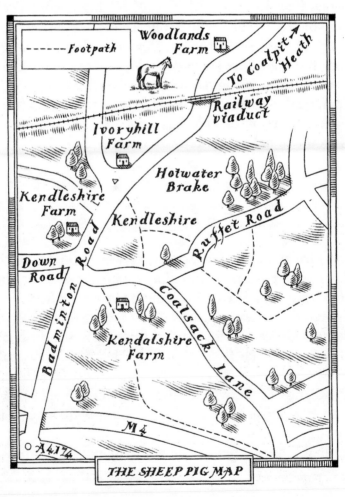

THE SHEEP PIG MAP

begins from the road, 100 yards before the viaduct.

Perhaps the most interesting spot for Babe-lovers is the village of Queen Charlton, five miles from Coalpit Heath, which each June holds a summer fair in the field near the church. It was for this fête many years ago that Dick King-Smith provided the prize pig for the 'guess the weight of the pig' competition, and had the germ of an idea:

> *I wondered what might happen if the pig was won*
> *by someone who didn't offer him up for his wife's*
> *deep freeze, but allowed him to have a less than*
> *usual life. Pigs are very clever animals – creatures of*
> *superior intelligence. You can teach them anything.*
> *(Dick King-Smith to author)*

If you visit the fête you may even be able to spot the author himself, who still regularly attends.

To see some real live pigs there are two farms in the area to which visitors are admitted. St Werburgh's City Farm is situated on Watercress Road in Bristol, near the city end of the M32 motorway, and has an extensive range of pigs. Also excellent for pig-spotting is the Norwood Rare Breeds Farm at Norton St Philip, about 20 minutes' drive south of Bath. This 320-acre farm has over 30 rare and special breeds of cattle, sheep, goats, ponies, poultry and – of course – pigs. Be sure not to miss pig-feeding time!

FURTHER INFORMATION

St Werburgh's City Farm is open daily. Entrance is free.
Norwood Rare Breeds Farm is open from the end of March to
the end of September. Pig feeding takes place every day.

THE RAILWAY CHILDREN
by E Nesbit

The 1970 film of *The Railway Children* (starring Jenny Agutter as Bobbie) has become such a firm family favourite that it is now hard to separate it from the book. When published in 1906, the novel was a strikingly different sort of children's story. At a time when many books were offering children comfortable tales of fairies and elves, *The Railway Children* tackled a much more serious situation. It tells of how a mother and three children manage to get by when the father is arrested and wrongfully imprisoned. E Nesbit shows that money can't buy happiness. Companionship, good neighbours and, of course, a railway at the bottom of the garden, are among the best things in life.

★   ★   ★   ★   ★

THE STORY

The lives of three ordinary children, Roberta, Peter and Phyllis, are turned upside down one evening when the police come to arrest their father. Now very short of money, the family has to move to the country. They take a house called Three Chimneys near a railway line.

Mother is kept busy trying to make ends meet, constantly writing stories to sell. But luckily, the children find a friend – the railway at the bottom of the hill.

Here in the deep silence of the sleeping country the only things that went by were the trains. They seemed to be all that was left to link the children to the old life that had once been theirs.

The people who work for the railway – and, later, the people who ride on it – fill their days with adventure and companionship. One particular railway traveller, the Old Gentleman who rides the 'Green Dragon', turns out to be a very special friend. By regularly waving to him, they form a firm friendship. He provides help when their mother falls ill. And when a Russian refugee turns up at the station, he even manages to find their family.

The children spend most of their days near the track or at the station with Perks, the porter. Even after Peter is caught stealing coal (Peter sees it as coal mining), Perks becomes their best friend. The children plan a surprise birthday party for him.

One day, while out on a picnic, the children manage to prevent a terrible accident. There is a landslide which blocks the line and, with the 11.29 due any minute, a disaster seems inevitable. Showing great resourcefulness, the girls find a way of alerting the engine driver and the Railway Children get bravery awards.

*'Oh stop, stop, stop!' cried Bobbie. No one heard
her. At least Peter and Phyllis didn't, for the
oncoming rush of the train covered the sound of
her voice with a mountain of sound. But afterwards
she used to wonder whether the engine itself had not
heard her. It seemed almost as though it had – for it
slackened swiftly, slackened and stopped, not twenty
yards from the place where Bobbie's two flags
waved over the line.*

Towards the end of the story, Roberta, Phyllis and
Peter once again brush with danger when they save a
grammar school boy out on a paperchase. They find
him with a broken leg in the railway tunnel and take
him home to be looked after by Mother. Much to
their surprise, the young boy's grandfather comes to
visit and turns out to be 'their own Old Gentleman'.
Life at Three Chimneys is never quite the same again
after his visit. The Old Gentleman, grateful for their
kindness to his grandson, returns the favour in the
most wonderful way.

E NESBIT

E Nesbit (the 'E' stands for Edith, but she was always
called Daisy) was born in 1858. She enjoyed a very
unconventional childhood, which she describes in a
fascinating book called *Long Ago When I Was Young*.
She was a difficult, quick-tempered child, happiest
when playing rough-and-tumble games with her
brothers. Her family travelled abroad, requiring the

young Edith to attend a succession of different schools, where she was troublesome and unhappy.

As a grown-up, Edith was as colourful and as unconventional as she was when she was a child. She smoked roll-up cigarettes, for instance, which at that time was a habit unknown among women in polite society.

At the age of 21, Edith was married to Hubert Bland. Shortly afterwards, her husband nearly died of small-pox and his business partner vanished with Hubert's money. Like Mother in *The Railway Children*, Edith was forced to provide for her family by writing stories. She was successful as a writer but didn't become well-known until 1898 when, at the age of 40, she produced a series of best-selling books beginning with *The Story of the Treasure Seekers*. The money provided by the *Treasure Seekers* allowed the family to move to a large house in Kent. It was here that she completed *The Railway Children*, and though the setting of the story isn't specified in the book, it is most likely the Kent countryside. (Characters in the story regularly travel up and down to London.) When director Lionel Jeffries looked for a location for his film he found the perfect place: the Worth Valley in Yorkshire.

Edith Nesbit died in 1924. A poem written after her death by C L Graves compared her with Hans Christian Andersen, 'the Prince of all the good magicians'.

THE TOUR

Though the scenery of the Worth Valley in Yorkshire is marvellous, this isn't what attracted director Lionel Jeffries to make the classic film of *The Railway Children* here. What lured him was the Keighley and Worth Valley Railway, a branch line hit by Dr Beeching's axe in the sixties but happily still thriving today in the hands of enthusiasts.

The places shown in the film, including the railway, still remain more or less just as they were in the film 25 years ago. Perks's wonderful station and even Three Chimneys, the children's home, are still there. To visit them now is wonderfully dreamlike, and *Railway Children* pilgrims can follow a Railway Children Walk which takes in the main locations for the film. But before taking the walk, you should first ride on the railway itself.

The three-minute train ride from Haworth to Oakworth station is packed with the adventures of the story. You pass through Mytholmes Tunnel, where Jim the schoolboy injured his leg whilst running in the paperchase. And to the left of the tunnel is where the landslide endangers the 11.29 train until the children save the day by waving pieces torn from their red flannel petticoats.

You will arrive at Oakworth station, where Perks once presided (played in the film by Bernard Cribbins). The railway preservation society has done a wonderful job

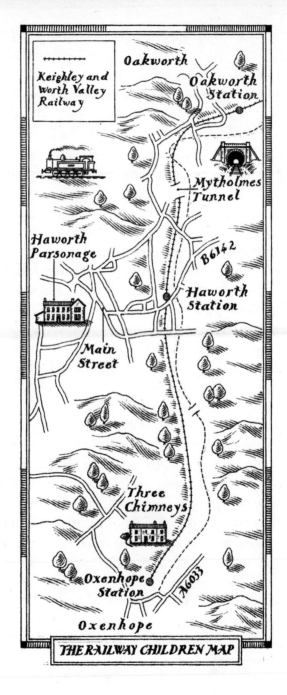

THE RAILWAY CHILDREN MAP

restoring the place to its pre-First World War state complete with gas lighting, tin platform advertisements and a roaring log fire in the waiting room. You could happily linger here for hours watching trains come and go. (Steam and 'heritage' diesel trains operate the 25-minute journey between Keighley and Oxenhope.) The place is a dream come true for anyone who has ever owned a Hornby train set.

From Oakworth it's a 20-minute walk up to the village of Haworth. Haworth parsonage, the real-life home of the Brontë family, was Dr Forrest's house in the film. A path leads down from the 'wuthering heights' of Haworth to the village of Oxenhope, at the end of the Worth Valley line. A short walk up from Oxenhope station, across the railway line, will bring you to the Three Chimneys of the film, Bents Farm. Walking away from the farm, down the field, you can re-live the closing moments of the story, when the children's father at last returns home:

He goes in and the door is shut. I think we will not open the door or follow him. I think that just now we are not wanted there. I think it will be best for us to go quickly and quietly away. At the end of the field, among the thin gold spikes of grass and the harebells and Gipsy roses and St John's Wort, we may just take one last look, over our shoulders, at the white house where neither we nor anyone else is wanted now.

THE LION, THE WITCH AND THE WARDROBE

by C S Lewis

When he was about 16 years old, an imaginary picture came into C S Lewis's mind of a faun carrying an umbrella and parcels in a snowy wood. This image stayed with him until later life, when, at the age of forty, he decided to write a story about it. And so began *The Lion, the Witch and the Wardrobe* – the first of seven books that make up *The Chronicles of Narnia*.

If a picture of a mythical creature carrying an umbrella and parcels seems an unlikely starting point for a book, then it has to be said that C S Lewis was probably one of the least likely children's authors. Aged over 50 when the book was published, Lewis was an unmarried teacher of English literature at Oxford University, and best known for writing books about religion. Asked why he'd written for children, C S Lewis replied simply, 'People won't write the books I want, so I have to do it for myself. . .'

Like Lewis Carroll, another Oxford University teacher, C S Lewis found Wonderland – though his was through the back of a family wardrobe.

THE STORY

It is wartime and Peter, Susan, Edmund and Lucy have been evacuated to the country to escape the air raids. They are sent to live with Professor Kirke, whose house is full of unexpected places which the children enjoy exploring.

One of the rooms they visit is empty, except for a wardrobe. When Lucy opens it and climbs in, a curious thing happens. Pushing her way through the fur coats in the enormous wardrobe, she finds that the back of the wardrobe is non-existent. Suddenly she finds herself in the middle of a dark snowy wood. Walking on, she discovers a lamp-post and then hears footsteps. Coming along a path towards her is a strange-looking person carrying parcels and an umbrella. He is Mr Tumnus, a faun, who has the upper half of a man and the legs and tail of a goat. He tells Lucy that she is in the Land of Narnia.

Friendly Mr Tumnus takes Lucy home for tea, but then, bursting into tears, admits to her that he is a spy for the evil White Witch. He tells Lucy that the White Witch has total power in Narnia and it is she who makes it always winter:

Always winter and never Christmas; think of that!

Mr Tumnus is under orders from the White Witch to keep watch for any humans, known as 'Sons of Adam or Daughters of Eve' in Narnia. He decides not to betray Lucy, however, and takes her back to the spot in the wood where he found her.

Lucy returns through the wardrobe, but everyone refuses to believe her story. Later on, during a game of hide-and-seek, Lucy again climbs into the wardrobe and this time Edmund follows her. He meets the White Witch, and, after gorging himself with enchanted Turkish Delight, tells her about Lucy, Susan and Peter. He also lets her know about Lucy's visit to Mr Tumnus. The Witch, who calls herself the Queen of Narnia, lays plans to lure them to her castle.

Some days later, in an attempt to dodge the house-keeper, all four children clamber into the wardrobe and find themselves in Narnia. They are horrified to find that the wolves of the White Witch's Secret Police have ransacked Mr Tumnus's home, taking him prisoner. The children follow a friendly robin to the safety of Mr and Mrs Beaver's house, who explain that Aslan, the good and great Lion, is on the move. They begin to make preparations to go to meet him at the ancient site of the Stone Table, when they discover that Edmund has run away to find the White Witch and has betrayed them all.

Edmund reaches her palace and finds it full of creatures she has turned into stone statues. The Witch dashes to face Aslan at the Stone Table, furious to find that her power is being weakened. Aslan's return has brought a winter thaw and the warmth of spring is returning. Even Father Christmas has paid a visit.

Wrong will be right, when Aslan comes in sight,
At the sound of his roar, sorrows will be no more,
When he bares his teeth, winter meets its death,
And when he shakes his mane, we shall have
spring again.

The Witch lays claim to the traitor Edmund's blood, and Aslan allows himself to be sacrificed in his place at the Stone Table. But by the secret Deep Magic, Aslan returns to life, rescuing all the creatures who have been turned to stone and rousing his army. A great battle follows, during which the White Witch is defeated. The four children are crowned Kings and Queens of Narnia at Cair Paravel.

Many years later, while on a royal hunting expedition in the woods, the now-adult Peter, Susan, Edmund and Lucy are intrigued to find a strange lamp-post in the middle of the trees. They follow a path which takes them back through the wardrobe, where they find that no time has passed at all . . .

And the next moment they all came tumbling out of
a wardrobe door into the empty room, and they
were no longer Kings and Queens in their hunting
array, but just Peter, Susan, Edmund and Lucy in
their old clothes.

C S LEWIS

Clive Staples Lewis was known simply as Jack, a name he chose for himself when he was only four! Born in Belfast, Northern Ireland, on 29 November 1898, he loved telling his own stories from an early age. Jack's older brother Warnie recalled how they used to sit together in the dark in an old oak wardrobe while Jack told tales of adventure. At the age of eight, Jack invented his own country: Animal Land, a place with a colourful array of animal characters such as a frog field-marshal named Sir Big. At the age of 10, his mother died and shortly afterwards he was sent to England to boarding school.

After fighting in the First World War, where he was wounded by shrapnel, Jack graduated from Oxford University and stayed on to work as a tutor. During the 1930s he wrote a number of successful books about English literature and also about Christianity.

In 1939, the year of the outbreak of the Second World War, a number of children evacuated from London stayed at Jack Lewis's house, The Kilns. One of the evacuees asked Jack if there was anything behind his large wardrobe. The question reminded him of the days long ago when he and Warnie had sat inside the wardrobe telling stories. But it wasn't until three years after the War that he began writing *The Lion, the Witch and the Wardrobe*, published in 1950 and eventually followed by six other Narnia books.

Jack married Joy Gresham, an American woman, in 1956. The dramatic story of their life together is told in the film *Shadowlands,* starring Anthony Hopkins and Debra Winger. Joy tragically died in July 1960, and Jack died three years later on 22 November 1963.

★　★　★　★　★

THE TOUR

Begin – where else? – at Lewis Close in Oxford. You might imagine that someone like C S Lewis would have lived in a very grand house, next door to one of the handsome college buildings. In fact, it is a great surprise to discover that his house, The Kilns, lies in a cul-de-sac in a very ordinary part of the city, just off the A4142 eastern bypass.

Most of the houses you see now were built after C S Lewis came to live here; originally, The Kilns would have been surrounded by countryside and of course the pottery which gave the house its name. If you think the house looks a little shabby today, it hasn't changed much since Jack Lewis and his brother lived there. Friends described it as a house built with books and held together by cobwebs. Despite the lack of a plaque on the wall to record its famous resident, many hundreds of people still come here every year to look at the house which once contained the famous wardrobe. A Californian foundation is planning to restore the building with the aim of converting it into an international study centre. It is also planning to recover the original wardrobe that inspired the book.

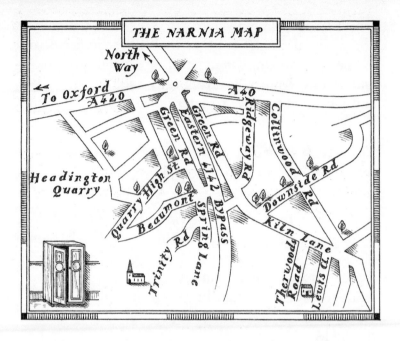

Just across the bypass from Kiln Lane is Headington Quarry, where C S Lewis is buried in the Holy Trinity Church. (To find his grave, stand with your back to the church door: his tombstone lies about 50 yards in front of you, between two tree trunks.) Inside the church is a lovely Narnia window, handsomely executed in etched glass.

Returning to the centre of Oxford, search out the Eagle and Child pub in St Giles (known locally as the 'Bird and Babe') where Lewis, *Lord of the Rings* author J R R Tolkien, and other members of the famous group known as the 'Inklings' used to meet. The local Lewis Society still holds gatherings there.

ROB ROY
by Sir Walter Scott

T hanks to Hollywood, we have come to know Rob Roy as a sort of Robin Hood in a kilt; Scotland's answer to the Sherwood Forest outlaw who stole from the rich and gave to the poor. But while there is a big question over the actual existence of Robin Hood, there is no doubt that Rob Roy MacGregor was a genuine historical figure. Indeed, when the young Sir Walter Scott travelled through the Trossachs he spoke to many people who had in fact met Rob Roy.

For Sir Walter, too, Rob Roy was a Highland hero, though it seems more likely that he was actually something of a villain. Rob's MacGregor clan were reported to have run a protection racket and their activities are meant to have given rise to the term 'blackmail'. But life in Scotland 300 years ago was necessarily harsh and ruthless. And we should not forget that, as England went to war with Bonnie Prince Charlie 10 years after Rob Roy's death, many of the English were determined to blacken the name of the Scots and present Rob Roy as a villain. Whatever the true story, a tour of the places connected with Rob Roy's life offers a trip through one of the loveliest parts of Britain.

125

THE STORY

The story is set in Scotland in 1715. German-born King George I had been invited to rule England after the death of Queen Anne, and the deposed King James II had fled to France. However, his son maintained hopes of returning to Britain to reclaim the throne, which resulted in the first major Jacobite rising against the English in 1715. The action therefore takes place during turbulent times.

Our narrator is Francis Osbaldistone, the son of a rich London merchant, who at the start of the novel refuses to accept his father's offer of employment in the family business.

> *. . . I stood fast, and, as respectfully as I could, declined the proposal he made to me.*

Francis is therefore sent to the north of England to live with his uncle, Sir Hildebrande Osbaldistone – a lover of fox-hunting and drinking. One of Sir Hildebrande's six sons, the cunning and deceitful Rashleigh, has been chosen to take the position in the business which Francis turned down.

> *'By the general wish to get Rashleigh out of the house,' replied Miss Vernon. 'Although, youngest of the family, he has somehow or other got the entire management of all the others; and every one is sensible of the subjection, though they cannot shake it off. If any one opposes him, he is sure to rue having done so . . .'*

This immediately causes Rashleigh to come into conflict with Francis. The situation worsens as Rashleigh has designs on Francis's sweetheart, Diana Vernon (Sir Hildebrande's neice). Rashleigh plots to destroy Francis and ruin Francis's father, taking the fortune for himself. However, Francis goes with Mr. Nicol Jarvie to seek the help of Rob Roy. Francis is present at a clash between Rob Roy and the royal troops, from which Rob makes a dramatic escape.

Indeed, as I partly suspected at the time, and afterwards learned with certainty, many of those who seemed most active in their attempts to waylay and recover the fugitive, were, in actual truth, least desirous that he should be taken, and only joined in the cry to increase the general confusion, and to give Rob Roy a better opportunity of escaping.

The villainous Rashleigh is made to give back the money he has stolen and is finally killed by Rob Roy. Francis makes peace with his father, marries Diana, and becomes the owner of the ancestral home, Osbaldistone Hall.

While the historical events are largely true, the characters are mostly invented – with the notable exception of Rob Roy and his wife. (In Gaelic, the language of the Scots, Rob Roy means 'Red Robert'; he was reported to have had red hair.) Robert MacGregor was born in 1671 and, at the age of 22, became the head of the MacGregor clan. Their land beside Loch Lomond lay between that of two powerful neighbours: the Dukes of Montrose and

Argyle. Rob became caught up in the strife between the two Dukes – one a supporter of the Jacobite cause, the other a supporter of George I. A particular quarrel between the Duke of Montrose and Rob Roy over a debt of £1000 led to Rob Roy being unjustly branded an outlaw.

Sir Walter portrays Rob as a shining example of honourable Highland tradition. He is described as the last great leader of a clan system that was being wiped out by 'civilised' Lowland administrators, who placed commerce and industry ahead of honour and courage. *Rob Roy* is the story of the clash between the old and the new.

SIR WALTER SCOTT

Though less well-known and less widely-read than other writers of the 1800s, Sir Walter Scott was the first man to earn a fortune from his writings. Today, he is seen as a writer of books which are mainly read by young people. However, during his lifetime, his books were enthusiastically enjoyed by everybody, including royalty.

Sir Walter Scott was born in 1771, the son of an Edinburgh lawyer. As a child he became fascinated by colourful stories of his ancestors' lives in the Border country between Scotland and England. Scott went on to study law, though his real interest lay in writing. He began with poetry, notably *The Lady of the Lake* in 1810.

Scott accrued mounting debts, partly through lavish spending on his extraordinary stately home, Abbotsford, situated on the River Tweed near Melrose. Eventually these totalled £130,000, which in today's value would amount to many millions of pounds. It was his failing financial situation which led him to produce a series of best-selling historical novels. These were mostly about Scotland, including *Waverley* and *The Heart of Midlothian*, though some were about English history. The most famous of its time was *Ivanhoe*, which sold out within a week of its publication in 1819, though *Rob Roy* is probably the best known of his books today.

In 1820 Sir Walter Scott's popularity led to his being made a baronet by King George IV. His novels were also translated into many languages and their success influenced generations of writers from Dickens to Tolstoy. Sir Walter died in 1832 and was buried in Dryburgh Abbey.

THE TOUR

Situated about an hour's drive north of Glasgow, the Trossachs is an area of outstanding beauty: all sparkling lochs, foaming rivers, purple-headed mountains and wild moors. It has been described as the Highlands in miniature and is a stretch of countryside that fires the imagination: 'So wond'rous wild, the whole might seem, the scenery of a faery dream.' You can see what Sir Walter Scott meant when you reach the small town of Callander, the starting point for the area of Scotland now known as 'Rob Roy Country'.

In Ancaster Square, Callander, you will find the excellent Rob Roy and Trossachs Visitor Centre. The upstairs audio-visual exhibition provides a fascinating background to the story; you can listen to a cast of characters, including Rob Roy himself, and also hear famous critical views about the Scottish hero from the likes of Daniel Defoe.

Next visit Rob Roy's birthplace: Glengyle, at the head of Loch Katrine, which is about 17 km west of Callander. You can explore the loch on a lovely old steamer called (what else?) the SS *Sir Walter Scott*, which sedately travels up and down the lake. At Portnellan, on the banks of the loch, is the house that Rob lived in after his marriage to Mary of Comar.

About 20 minutes' drive south of Callander is, without doubt, the prettiest place associated with Rob Roy: Balquhidder. It was here that Rob Roy spent his last days. When his end drew near in December 1734, it is said he called out:

Now all is over. Put me to bed. Call the Piper. Let him play 'Cha till mi tuille', for my time is come.

130

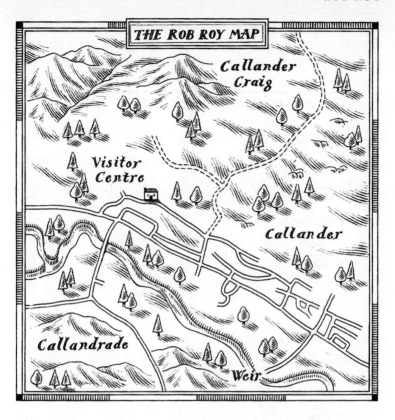

THE ROB ROY MAP

Callander Craig

Visitor Centre

Callander

Callandrade

Weir

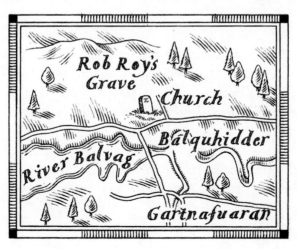

Rob Roy's Grave

Church

Balquhidder

River Balvag

Gartnafuaran

The piper played the old lament 'I shall return no more' as Rob Roy died in his house at Inverlochlarig Beg. Rob is buried in a simple grave with his wife Mary and two of his four sons – the modern inscription on the grave reads 'MacGregor Despite Them'.

If you have the time, don't forget to visit Sir Walter Scott's house, Abbotsford, (near Melrose), which is now a fascinating museum. In the house's library you will find an exciting collection of Scottish memorabilia including Rob Roy's very own purse and knife.

WINNIE-THE-POOH
by A A Milne

The tales of 'a Bear of Very Little Brain', his friend Christopher Robin, and the other Animals of the Forest: Piglet, Eeyore, Rabbit, Owl, Kanga and Roo, have been an enduring children's favourite since *Winnie-The-Pooh* was published in 1926. Over 70 years the book has been translated into more than 30 languages, including Bulgarian, Czech, Russian and even Latin, with sales running into millions of copies.

But while *Winnie-the-Pooh* may have been the product of the imagination of the author A A Milne, the landscape his characters inhabit is quite real. A short distance from the attractive Sussex village of Hartfield, Pooh's world still remains more or less as E H Shepard, the illustrator, drew it in the 1920s. Visitors to Pooh Country can play Poohsticks on the real Poohsticks bridge, linger in Eeyore's Gloomy Place, and see Rabbit's home – where Pooh was once 'a Wedged Bear in Great Tightness'.

★　　★　　★　　★　　★

THE STORY

The adventures of Winnie-the-Pooh and his friends take place in the Hundred Acre Wood, where they live. Luckily, Christopher Robin's house is also nearby, as he is often needed to come to their rescue.

When we first meet Pooh, he is trying to sneak some of his much-loved honey from beneath the noses of a swarm of very suspicious and angry bees. He disguises himself as a little black rain cloud and floats on the end of a blue balloon up to the honeycomb. But how is Pooh going to get down again?

Pooh's love for honey (and condensed milk) lands him in further trouble when he visits Rabbit in the second story. Pooh's waistline expands so much that he ends up wedged in Rabbit's front door, forced to go on a sudden crash diet.

Piglet joins Pooh in the next chapter when they go walking together in the snow. They frighten themselves by thinking they may be on the tracks of some Woozles and maybe even a Wizzle (perhaps of hostile intent). But Christopher Robin manages to solve the puzzle of the mysteriously multiplying footprints. However, they're not so lucky later on, when Pooh and Piglet's efforts to trap a Heffalump produce more confusion:

> *'Help, help!' cried Piglet, 'a Heffalump, a Horrible Heffalump!' and he scampered off as hard as he could, still crying out, 'Help, help, a Herrible Hoffalump! Hoff, Hoff, a Hellible Horralump!'*

We first encounter Eeyore, the gloomy, old grey donkey, standing by himself in a thistly corner of the

Forest thinking about this and that. It is just Eeyore's luck that his tail has gone missing, though it turns out to be no coincidence that Owl has a handsome new bell-rope. When Eeyore's birthday is forgotten, Pooh organises some surprises. Eeyore is not disappointed, even though Pooh absent-mindedly eats his present and Piglet bursts the balloon he was planning to give.

Kanga and Roo cause consternation when they arrive in the Forest, as nobody knows where they have come from. But they are quickly accepted and join Christopher Robin's 'Expotition' to discover the North Pole. Shortly afterwards, the forest is flooded. Pooh escapes to Christopher Robin's house by sitting on a floating honey jar, while Piglet is rescued by using an upturned umbrella. Christopher Robin invites everybody to a party for Pooh to thank him for saving Piglet, and Pooh is delighted to receive a special award.

Pooh and friends, by E H Shepard.

It was a Special Pencil Case. There were pencils in it marked 'B' for Bear, and pencils marked 'HB' for Helping Bear, and pencils marked 'BB' for Brave Bear.

A A MILNE

A A Milne always expected to be remembered as a playwright, as in the early 1920s he enjoyed fantastic success in London's West End and on New York's Broadway. But today we remember him for only one play, *Toad of Toad Hall* – an adaptation of his favourite book: Kenneth Grahame's *The Wind in the Willows*. In fact, Milne owes his current fame to a toy bear bought from Harrods for his only son, Christopher Robin, born in 1920. The bear was named 'Pooh' after a swan Milne and his son had once met on an outing. The name 'Winnie' came from a bear in London Zoo which Christopher Robin loved (so called because it had been brought by a First World War soldier from Winnipeg in Canada).

Alan Milne was born in London in 1882, the youngest of a public school headmaster's three sons. He won scholarships to Westminster School and then Trinity College, Cambridge, where he edited the student magazine *Granta*. After university, he became assistant editor of *Punch*, before serving in the army during the First World War.

Milne then turned to writing plays, and, because of his great success, was able in 1925 to buy a weekend country house near the village of Hartfield, on the edge of Ashdown Forest. Cotchford Farm was used mainly as a weekend retreat. The young Christopher Robin would leave the Milnes' London home in Chelsea with his collection of soft toys: Pooh, Eeyore, Piglet, Tigger, Kanga and Roo. It was watching

Christopher Robin wandering the local countryside with his toys that provided Milne with the inspiration for the book.

Christopher Robin and Pooh actually make their first literary appearance in 1924, in a book of poetry called *When We Were Very Young*. The next book, *Winnie-the-Pooh*, was published in 1926 and quickly

Kanga in Ashdown Forest, illustrated by E H Shepard.

became a bestseller, both in Britain and in America. This was followed by another book of poems in 1927, *Now We Are Six*, and the last of the Pooh books in 1928, *The House at Pooh Corner*.

A A Milne continued to live at Cotchford Farm until his death in January 1956. But nothing he ever wrote after 1928 proved so popular, causing the author some regret. The success of the books also proved a mixed blessing for Christopher Robin, who grew up to run a successful Devon bookshop but found that people wanted to remember him as a six-year-old boy with a toy bear. The original toy animals owned by Christopher Robin: Winnie-the-Pooh, Piglet, Eeyore and Kanga (Roo was lost), are on view at the New York Public Library in America.

THE TOUR

The home of all the 'Animals of the Forest', can be found between East Grinstead and Tunbridge Wells, at the village of Hartfield in Sussex. A useful map, showing you the main places connected with the book, is sold at the Pooh Corner shop in Hartfield itself. The map was produced by Maire McQueeney, who leads walks through 'Pooh country' several times a year.

One of the best places to begin is at Pooh Car Park near Chuck Hatch, a short drive south-west of Hartfield. Nearby, in a sandy bank, you can find Rabbit's house with its front and back doors. It's here that Pooh ate too much honey and condensed milk and became wedged in the front door as he tried to leave. For a week, until Pooh lost weight again and could be pulled out, Christopher Robin read a Sustaining Book at the North End of Pooh while Rabbit hung his washing on Pooh's South End.

It's a short walk to Poohsticks bridge where Pooh invented the game of Poohsticks by dropping fir cones

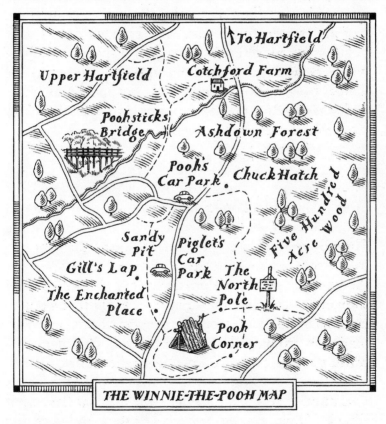

THE WINNIE-THE-POOH MAP

into the water and seeing which one appeared first on the other side. (Fir cones were quickly replaced by sticks because they were easier to find.) The bridge has been carefully preserved to look just as E H Shepard drew it, with the wooden rails on which Christopher Robin is illustrated, standing and leaning over to drop his stick in the water. If you look downstream, you'll see that the water is choked with a thick tangle of 'dead' Poohsticks. (About 15 minutes' walk from the bridge is Cotchford Farm, the Milne family's house, though this is not open to the public.)

For the other Pooh places, the best parking spot is Piglet's car park. From here, it is a 10-minute walk down the hillside to the North Pole. For Pooh, the Pole in question was not the axis upon which the earth revolved. On their 'Expotition', the Pole turns out to be a useful stick which is used to fish Roo out of the stream.

A path leads up open heath towards the Five Hundred Acre Wood – in *Pooh,* the Hundred Acre Wood. En route you can see Pooh Corner (where Eeyore's house is built) and the Sandy Pit where Roo played.

The final port of call on the tour is the Enchanted Place. Near here, at Gill's Lap, is a memorial to Milne and Shepard 'who collaborated in the creation of Winnie-the-Pooh and so captured the magic of Ashdown Forest and gave it to the world'. Here amongst the pine trees is where Milne leaves Christopher Robin and Winnie-the-Pooh at the end of *The House at Pooh Corner.* The tale is over because Christopher Robin is about to go to school. But of course, as Milne writes, the story is never over:

*Wherever they go and whatever happens to them
on the way, in that enchanted place on the top
of the Forest, a little boy and his Bear will
always be playing.*

And with the Pooh books continuing to sell as well as ever, Pooh and Christopher will continue to play in the Forest for a very long time.

FURTHER INFORMATION

The Pooh Corner Shop in Hartfield offers a wide range of books, presents and gifts – as well as Pooh's Forest map.
Maire McQueeney's Twentieth Century Walks runs regular *Pooh* walks throughout the year.
The Ashdown Forest Centre and Wealden Tourist Information Office can give you more information about the area.

A CHRISTMAS CAROL
by *Charles Dickens*

I have endeavoured in this Ghostly little book, to raise the Ghost of an Idea . . . May it haunt their house pleasantly, and no one wish to lay it.
(CHARLES DICKENS, THE PREFACE TO *A CHRISTMAS CAROL*)

Of all Charles Dickens's wonderful books, it is *A Christmas Carol* which is perhaps the best loved and most widely enjoyed, having become as much a part of our annual Christmas festivities as crackers and streamers. In fact, some say that the book has actually helped to shape the way we have come to celebrate Christmas.

The story of a mean old man who discovers the pleasure of giving still moves us, perhaps because Dickens himself felt so strongly about it. It is said that he both laughed and wept over writing it. As the story took shape in his mind, he tramped alone through London's streets at night, covering as many as 15 miles at a time. In those night-time wanderings, he no doubt passed along the very streets that you will walk along if you go in search of the real locations of the book.

★ ★ ★ ★ ★

THE STORY

From its very first line, *A Christmas Carol* holds us in its delightful grip.

> *Marley was dead: to begin with. There is no doubt whatever about that.*

Scrooge sees Ignorance and Want. Illustration by John Leech.

It is Christmas Eve and old Ebenezer Scrooge is busy in his counting house. Outside it is cold, bleak and foggy. Inside, Scrooge's clerk, Bob Cratchit, is shivering over a tiny fire. A cheerful voice interrupts the proceedings. It's Scrooge's nephew with an invitation to Christmas dinner, but Scrooge rejects this sourly. Christmas and all its trimmings are 'Humbug' to Scrooge. All he wants is to be left alone.

> *... every idiot who goes about with 'Merry Christmas' on his lips, should be boiled with his own pudding, and buried with a stake of holly through his heart.*

After Scrooge returns to his gloomy home, he is paid a visit by some unexpected guests. First comes the transparent ghost of Jacob Marley, Scrooge's dead partner, who drags a chain of cash registers, keys and padlocks. He has come to prepare the way for three further spirits that are to follow.

The first is the Ghost of Christmas Past. This spirit reminds Scrooge of the childhood Christmases which he spent lonely, neglected by his family and friends. Next is the Ghost of Christmas Present. Scrooge is taken to Bob Cratchit's house, where the family are happily celebrating Christmas Day despite the small salary that Bob receives from Scrooge. They see Cratchit's son, Tiny Tim, who is very ill. The third and final visitor is the Ghost of Christmas Yet To Come. It is from this spirit that Scrooge learns his most shocking lesson: after his death he will be missed by no one.

The haunting by these three spirits transforms Scrooge. He promises to alter his life and make sure that the dismal future he was shown will not come about. He throws open the window. The Christmas bells are ringing out and the sun is shining. Scrooge shouts to a small boy to go to the Poulterer's and buy the biggest turkey, then to take it to Bob Cratchit's house.

'A merry Christmas, Bob!', said Scrooge, with an earnestness that could not be mistaken, as he clapped him on the back. 'A merrier Christmas, Bob, my good fellow, than I have given you, for many a year!'

Scrooge vows to honour Christmas every day of the year. He gives Bob a rise in salary and more coal for his fire, also becoming a second father to Tiny Tim. Scrooge never sees any more spirits but it was always said of him that he knew how to keep Christmas well!

★   ★   ★   ★   ★

CHARLES DICKENS

Charles Dickens was born in Portsmouth in 1812. His father, a naval pay clerk, was frequently in financial difficulties and eventually ended up in the Marshalsea debtors' prison in London. The family's lack of money meant that, at the age of 12, Charles was sent to work in a black-leading warehouse, sticking labels on bottles for ten hours a day, six days a week.

Charles eventually returned to school for a short time, and at 15 started work in a lawyer's office. He then embarked on a career in newspapers as a shorthand reporter. It was during this time that he began work on his first novel, *The Pickwick Papers,* which turned out to be an almost instant success. *Pickwick* was quickly followed by *Oliver Twist, Nicholas Nickleby, The Old Curiosity Shop* and *Barnaby Rudge.* By 1843, just seven years after writing *Pickwick,* Dickens was the most popular author in Britain.

However, despite his success, Dickens was short of money. He hurried to complete *A Christmas Carol* in just six weeks so that it could be published in time for Christmas. The story harks back to the troubled times of Dickens's own childhood. The poverty-stricken Cratchit family in one of Camden's small terraced houses bear a striking resemblance to Dickens's own family, who also lived in Camden Town. Dickens also had a crippled brother known, not as 'Tiny Tim', but as 'Tiny Fred'.

Dickens made plans to publish the story in a handsome cover with gilt-edged pages and full-colour etchings, at the relatively modest price of five shillings. But while it was the best-selling book of the Christmas period, unhappily, Dickens saw little profit. As was common at the time, a 'pirated' edition of the book was published. Dickens sued for breach of copyright and won. But the pirate publishers and printers declared themselves bankrupt, leaving Dickens with a bill of £700. As a result, the £1000 profit he had hoped for turned out to be nearer £130. Dickens immediately feared that, like his father, he too might end up in the debtors' prison: 'I shall be ruined past all mortal hope of redemption,' he wrote. In fact, Dickens went on to achieve further success, producing what are reckoned to be his greatest works, including *Dombey and Son*, *David Copperfield*, *Bleak House*, *Hard Times*, *Little Dorrit*, *A Tale of Two Cities*, *Great Expectations* and *Our Mutual Friend*.

Towards the end of his life, Dickens earned more money and fame from giving public readings of his books, particularly the ever-popular *A Christmas Carol*. Dickens was a restless traveller throughout his life, forever on the move. He died of a brain haemorrhage at the age of 58, and it was said that even as he lay dying, he was muttering about plans for travelling to London.

THE TOUR

Despite the devastation wreaked by the Blitz in the Second World War, you can still see much of the London that Dickens and Scrooge would have known so well. Clues to actual locations are sprinkled throughout the tale of *A Christmas Carol*, and it takes only a little detective work to identify several of the places Dickens had in mind when writing the story.

We are told that Scrooge's counting house lies on a court in the vicinity of Cornhill. (After the office closes, Bob Cratchit goes down a slide on Cornhill 20 times 'in honour of its being Christmas Eve'.) And opposite the counting house is: 'the ancient tower of a church, whose gruff old bell was always peeping slily down at Scrooge out of a gothic window in the wall'. Today, if you stand on Cornhill, opposite the ancient tower of the Church of St Michael's you will see Newman Court. It is easy to imagine a foggy Christmas Eve afternoon, with candles 'flaring in the windows of the neighbouring offices, like ruddy smears upon the palpable brown air'.

Scrooge, however, doesn't keep Christmas at all, but takes 'his melancholy dinner in his usual melancholy tavern'. Follow Scrooge's steps behind St Michael's Church, down St Michael's Alley to the Jamaica Wine

147

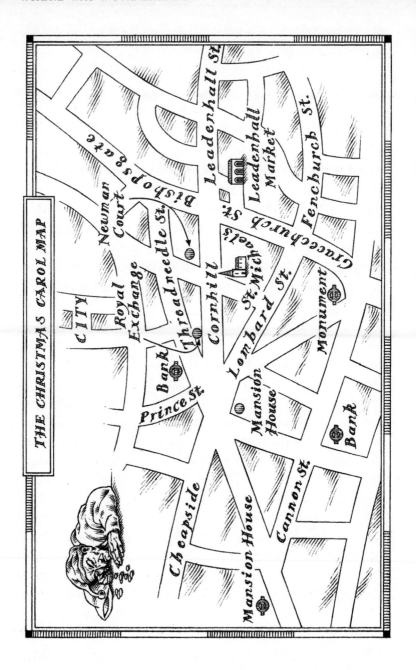

THE CHRISTMAS CAROL MAP

148

House. (This was built on the site of Pasqua Rosa's, which opened in 1652 as London's first coffee house.) Nearby, you will find Simpsons (with the curious address of 38 and a half Cornhill), the likely location of the gloomy Scrooge's favourite inn.

Next, return to Cornhill and continue west where the final spirit leads Scrooge to the Royal Exchange:

> *. . . amongst the merchants; who hurried up and down, and chinked the money in their pockets, and conversed in groups, and looked at their watches, and trifled thoughtfully with their great gold seals; and so forth, as Scrooge had seen them often.*

You can imagine the dismay Scrooge feels when he hears his fellow merchants discussing his death in an off-hand way. Across the road from the handsome Exchange building stands the Mansion House where the Lord Mayor '. . . gave orders to his fifty cooks and butlers to keep Christmas as a Lord Mayor's household should'. The Lord Mayor still resides here, though, presumably, he has to make do with far fewer staff.

Return up Cornhill and turn off to the right to Leadenhall Market. When Scrooge finds himself back in his bed on Christmas morning with a chance to make a fresh start, one of the first things he does is to instruct a passing boy to go to the Poulterer's 'in the next street but one' to buy a prize turkey for Bob Cratchit. This turkey would almost certainly have been bought at Leadenhall Market, a place Dickens knew well. Once at the centre of the Roman Forum, the market now sits in the shadow of the Lloyd's building, London's most famous piece of modern architecture. Leadenhall is a handsome covered market with attractive cream and maroon cast-ironwork. Here there would have been Poulterers a-plenty offering prize turkeys for Christmas. On a foggy winter's evening, as the lights flicker on, you may even glimpse the ghost of Bob Cratchit hurrying past on his way back home to his family in Camden Town.

CIDER WITH ROSIE
by Laurie Lee

L aurie Lee's wonderful account of his childhood in England's Cotswolds is officially classified as an autobiography, though he admits in an opening note that some of his memories may have been 'distorted' by the passing of time. *Cider With Rosie* is a strange and magical mixture of non-fiction and fiction, in which memories of real events and actual people blend indistinguishably with imagined happenings and characters. For instance, it has been suggested that the lovely Rosie herself is a character from Laurie Lee's imagination, though this is strongly denied by the author, who says that her identity is a secret he will take to his grave.

Laurie Lee's village of Slad can be found a few miles from the town of Stroud in Gloucestershire, just as he described it in his book. Here you will find the Lee family house, the schoolroom where he was tormented by his teacher, Crabby Bee, and the field where on one golden summer's afternoon he took cider with Rosie, kissing her beneath the hay wagon which 'went floating away like a barge, out over the valley . . .'.

THE STORY

Laurie's earliest memories start at the age of three, the final year of the First World War, and the time when his family moved to the village of Slad.

I was set down from the carrier's cart at the age of three: and there with a sense of bewilderment and terror my life in the village began.

He is fussed over by his big sisters, who flannel his face in the morning and feed him berries and currants from the garden. When the village hears that the War is finally over, bonfires are lit in celebration.

As Laurie grows older, he is no longer allowed to sleep in his mother's comfy bed. His growing awareness of the world is accompanied by a sense of unease. He has a frightening encounter with Jones's goat, and ghostly village stories fill his head about silver-grey stage-coaches and the hangman at Bulls Cross. Laurie remembers people scuttling to bolt their doors against the quirks of eccentric neighbours like Cabbage-Stump, and he recalls the drama of the flood after the summer drought of 1921.

Laurie survives his first day at school despite the sour headteacher, Crabby, who humiliates and goads the children. One day Spadge Hopkins rebels and becomes the hero of the school. By the end of his time at school Laurie has started to enjoy it – particularly writing.

Laurie describes his home life with his mother. He

remembers her love of old china and how on summer nights she would play the piano. He also clearly recalls the change of seasons. Winter is remembered as a time when the village boys help to feed Farmer Wells's calves and go sliding on Jones's pond. Before Christmas, when the snow lies thick, they go carol-singing with lanterns made from candles in marmalade jars. In turn, summer is described as a time when the heat from the ground climbs up Laurie's legs and the village is silent. He and his friends suck sherbet through sticks of liquorice and drink at the spring. The years pass by, with Laurie undergoing a life-changing experience when he spends an afternoon and evening with Rosie Burdock, kissing and drinking cider underneath a hay wagon.

The day Rosie Burdock decided to take me in hand was a motionless day of summer, creamy, hazy and amber-coloured, with the beech trees standing in heavy sunlight as though clogged with wild wet honey.

The end of Laurie's childhood coincides with the last days of traditional village life. Motor-cars and buses link the village directly with the outside world, and this has dramatic consequences. The last days of his family life also draw near as his sisters and brother Harold bring home prospective partners. Laurie sees that his future lies outside the valley and prepares for the world of adulthood.

LAURIE LEE

Laurie Lee was born in Stroud in 1914. He is not quite sure of the actual date, and when plans were laid to celebrate his 80th birthday, he admitted that his birth had never been registered by his mother. When questioned she could only remember that it was on a Thursday – as it was also early closing that day!

There were seven children in the family, three of them from Laurie's father's first marriage. His father, however, had already left his family, leaving Laurie's mother to raise all the children alone.

At the age of 15, Laurie took an office job in Stroud. Then in 1934, in the finest tradition of fairy stories, he decided to go up to London to seek his fortune, supporting himself by playing his fiddle and labouring on building sites. In 1935 he travelled to Spain, later returning during the country's Civil War to fight against the fascists. (He describes these experiences in his books *As I Walked Out One Midsummer Morning* and *A Rose for Winter*.) After the Second World War, Laurie spent around 15 years on the edges of London literary and artistic society before returning to the Gloucestershire countryside where his heart had always remained.

Throughout the 1950s Laurie Lee gained a reputation for his poetry, but it was the publication of *Cider with Rosie* in 1959 which made him a famous writer. One of the conditions under which the Hogarth Press agreed to publish the book was that the author should write his own advertising blurb for the back cover. Laurie Lee wrote 'Should become a classic' for his blurb. He was certainly proved right.

THE TOUR

Seen through the young Laurie Lee's eyes, Slad seems a place of substantial size. In fact, if you're not careful, you can easily shoot straight through the village by car before you have a chance to stop. But, providing this doesn't happen, you will find that an enjoyable 90-minute walk will enable you to experience most of the places described by Laurie Lee in *Cider with Rosie*.

After entering Slad, travel up the valley towards Painswick and pass the Woolpack Inn on your right. Stop a couple of hundred yards further on your right, at the top of a small road which leads down the hill, near a sign saying 'Steanbridge Lane'. Standing by the sign, look down to the foot of a steep bank and there in front of you is the cottage in which Laurie Lee lived from the age of three. Mrs Lee used to scramble up this slope to catch the bus to Stroud. And it was on this bank that Laurie played his doctor games with Jo. The T-shaped house with mullioned windows was known as Lee's Cottage when Laurie and his large family lived there. Now it is called Rosebank and is a private residence.

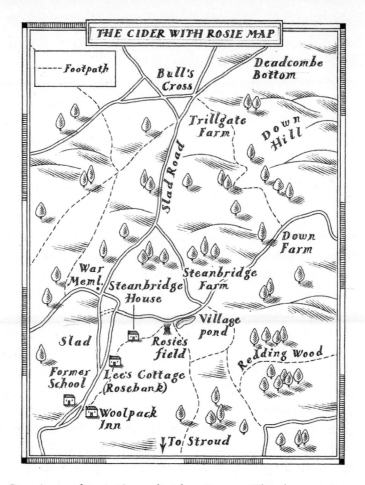

Continue down Steanbridge Lane. The large manor house you will see on your right is Steanbridge House, the 'Big House' of Squire Jones (owner of the much-feared goat). On Peace Day, Laurie came here in a procession dressed as John Bull and was given a prize by the Squire in the Big House gardens. A little further on is the village pond where Fred Bates, the milkman, discovered the naked body of Miss Flynn floating dead among the lily-weeds.

156

To find the place where a kiss changed Laurie Lee's life forever, follow the footpath which takes you off the road, skirting the pond at the village end and leading up the hill. The field to the right of the path is the very place where Laurie took cider with Rosie during haymaking, one beautiful summer's afternoon after school.

To share Laurie Lee's more sinister experiences of Slad, walk back down the lane past the pond, and after 200 yards a steep and rocky footpath will lead to the left, climbing the hill. A few hundred yards before reaching the road, take the path to the right which runs parallel to the road, skirting the trees. At Trillgate Farm, look down at the wood in the bottom of the valley. This is described in the book as Deadcombe Bottom, where the Bulls Cross hangman lived. If you turn to the left and climb up towards the road you will reach Bulls Cross itself, the site of the gallows where criminals were hanged. After 200 yards down the road returning to Slad, a path to the right leads through the woods and out into the village near the War Memorial. This is where the Slad man who had been to New Zealand and made good was killed by villagers who disliked the way he showed off about his success.

Turn to the right again and follow the road down to the Woolpack Inn. The private house opposite the inn was once the village school where Laurie Lee was a pupil. It is here that the young Laurie would have gazed out of the windows on the view of fields and hedgerows planted a thousand years ago.

THE HUNDRED AND ONE DALMATIANS

by Dodie Smith

This doggy detective story is one of those special books that can be equally enjoyed by readers of all ages. As well as being a popular book, *The Hundred and One Dalmatians* story has also been made into two films by Disney, an earlier animated version and a more recent live-action film, starring Glenn Close with a large collection of dalmatians.

It is often said that dogs are considerably more intelligent than the people who own them, and Pongo and Missis, the two canine stars of *The Hundred And One Dalmatians*, are certainly more than capable of looking after themselves. When their puppies are stolen by the evil Cruella de Vil they set off to rescue them, tracking them down to the heart of the English countryside.

It comes as no surprise that Dodie Smith herself was an avid dalmatian lover, owning no fewer than seven of them during her 94-year life! More surprising, however, is the trouble she took to place the story against a background of real-life settings. Anyone who has enjoyed the book will therefore have a special pleasure in tracing the actual places Dodie Smith describes so carefully.

THE STORY

Mr and Mrs Dearly live in a small but happy house in Regent's Park with their two Nannies and their beloved dalmatian dogs, Pongo and Missis Pongo. The dogs regard Mr and Mrs Dearly as their human pets, who are intelligent enough to understand a number of barks!

Like many other much-loved humans, they believed that they owned their dogs, instead of realising that their dogs owned them. Pongo and Missis found this touching and amusing and let their pets think it was true.

One day, after a beautiful evening's walk, the Dearlys' peace is shattered by an extremely loud motor horn. A lady gets out of the car whom Mrs Dearly recognises from her days at school: Cruella de Vil, someone she was rather scared of. Cruella has a rather odd appearance. One side of her hair is white, the other black, and she has a long pointed nose and red eyes. She is dressed in a long white fur cloak, and we later hear she sleeps in ermine sheets. Cruella displays a most sinister interest in the dogs.

When Missis gives birth to 15 puppies Cruella says she would like to buy them. However, Mr Dearly tells her firmly they are not for sale. The puppies' spots start to develop and they begin to get bigger every day. But one day when Mr Dearly is at work and Mrs Dearly is out walking with Pongo and Missis – horror – they are stolen! Cruella is the chief suspect.

The best efforts of the Dearlys and the police to track down the puppies achieve nothing. Pongo, however, with one of the keenest brains in Dogdom, hatches his own plan. On their evening walk, at the top of Primrose Hill, he and Missis bark a message about the stolen puppies. (All dogs know about the Twilight Barking – it's the way dogs keep up with old friends, important news or just gossip!) Pongo and Missis wait for news to be barked back and, at the last moment, a message is relayed from a Great Dane who tells them that their puppies are in Suffolk. Instructions are provided for finding the village, with offers of places to stay on the way.

Illustration by Janet and Anne
Grahame-Johnstone.

The puppies are being held at Hell Hall, ancestral home of the de Vils, where it seems that Cruella has plans to turn them into dalmatian fur coats!

> *'Listen,' said Cruella de Vil. 'I don't care how you kill the little beasts. Hang them, suffocate them, drop them off the roof – good gracious, there are dozens of lovely ways. I only wish I'd time to do the job myself.'*

When Pongo and Missis arrive at the Hall, they find not only their own puppies, but 99 dalmatians altogether. Pongo and Missis organise a great doggy escape and get themselves and all the rescued dalmatians safely back to London – 101 dalmatians in all.

DODIE SMITH

Dodie Smith was born on 3 May 1896 in Manchester, and from an early age was set on a theatre career. She relied entirely on her own abilities to make her way in life, as by the time she was 18 and studying to be an actress at London's Royal Academy of Dramatic Art, both her parents had died. Only 5ft tall and not especially handsome, she nevertheless found plenty of work acting in provincial theatres and seaside shows. However Dodie quickly realised that she would never make her name on the stage and, tiring of the hand-to-mouth theatre existence, she abandoned her acting career.

Dodie found work at Heal's, a famous London furniture store, earning £3 a week. It was while working here that she met her future husband, Alec Beesley, who provided the support Dodie needed while writing her first play, *Autumn Crocus*. Performed in 1931, it was an instant hit, making Dodie an overnight celebrity. She went on to become one of Britain's most successful playwrights in the Thirties with a string of hits including her best-known play, *Dear Octopus*.

With her new wealth, Dodie and Alec moved into a new flat in London's fashionable Dorset Square. The apartment was decorated in very stylish black and white, and Dodie joked, 'All I need now is a dalmatian.' Alec Beesley took her at her word, presenting her with a hatbox on her 38th birthday which contained a dalmatian puppy! Dodie called him Pongo, and this name was immortalised years later as the hero of *The Hundred and One Dalmatians*.

Dodie and Alec left England shortly before the start of the Second World War. Pongo accompanied them to Hollywood, where Dodie began a new life as a screenwriter. When Pongo died, Dodie replaced him with two new dalmatians, Folly and Buzz, who in 1943 gave birth to 15 puppies. (Just like Cadpig, there was one puppy which had to be nursed back to life.) In order to feed the huge brood, Alec found a dalmatian at the local pound who had recently lost her puppies – the original of Perdita in *The Hundred and One Dalmatians*.

Dodie and Alec eventually returned to England in 1953. Buzz grew so thin in the British quarantine kennels that he had to be treated by St John's Wood vet, Proby J Cautley, the model for the Splendid Vet in the story. Dodie's style of playwriting had gone out of fashion, but at the end of 1955, she decided to try her hand at writing a children's story. She had had a tale in mind for 20 years, since an actress friend, Joyce Kennedy, had first observed of Pongo, 'He would make a nice fur coat.' She completed the story in seven weeks and it was published in November 1956 to instant acclaim. Within a few months Walt Disney had bought the film rights (Walt himself called on Dodie in her Suffolk cottage) and the animated film opened for the Christmas holiday of 1961. Despite the fact that Disney had made changes to the story (for example, Mr Dearly, mathematical wizard, was reborn as Roger Ratcliffe, song writer), Dodie was largely delighted with the finished product.

Dodie Smith died in 1990 but her story looks as if it will live forever. It continues to find an audience with each new generation.

THE TOUR

On a first visit to London, people are always surprised by how many green open spaces there are in the city. Dodie Smith longed to live in one of the largest and probably the finest, Regent's Park, setting her heart on Number One St Andrew's Place, which is exactly on the corner of Outer Circle. The house is little more than five minutes' walk from Regent's Park or Great Portland Street tube station and the noise and bustle of Marylebone Road, but standing outside it, looking towards the park, you can easily imagine you are deep in the countryside. Dodie Smith made her private dream come true in print, as although she was never able to live in St Andrew's Place, the human heroes of *The Hundred And One Dalmatians* do.

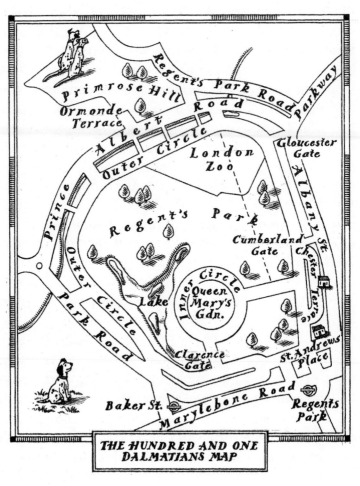

THE HUNDRED AND ONE
DALMATIANS MAP

The address isn't specified in the story, but as soon as you arrive at the handsome terraced house you know you are at the home of the Dearlys. Thanks to the careful and affectionate illustrations of the first edition (by Janet and Anne Grahame-Johnstone) if you visit St Andrew's Place today, it will all look instantly familiar. There are the characteristic street lamps, the neat iron railings, the columned cream-painted facade of the house and the basement area down into which the hapless Lucky was dropped by Cruella de Vil after nipping her ear. (Fortunately he landed in Nanny Butler's outstretched apron!) The place is just as Dodie Smith described it over 40 years ago.

If you plan to retrace the steps of Mr and Mrs Dearly, Pongo and Missis on one of their favourite walks to Primrose Hill, prepare yourself for a bit of a trek. From St Andrew's Place to the top of Primrose Hill is a stroll of some three miles there and back, but it's well worth the effort. As you walk up the Outer Circle, passing by the grand houses, you can speculate on which would have been the residence of the great composer heard by the Dearlys playing the piano as they pass by at the start of the novel. Soon, as Pongo and Missis did on their trek to Suffolk, you will pass by the famous London Zoo (it reminded Pongo of his wild ancestry and his liking for adventure). Over to the right is the Parkway and the bridge over the railway line from Euston station. Pongo and Missis stopped near this bridge, looking back along the curve of the Circle and thinking of the day when they would return with 15 puppies running behind them. (Little did they know it would be many more than that!)

Shortly afterwards, cross Prince Albert Road and enter Primrose Hill. Climb to the top of the hill for a glorious view of London's imposing skyline, then half-close your eyes and imagine Pongo and Missis here on that troubled evening after the shocking theft of their puppies. They went to the top of the hill, stood side by side and barked to the north, south, east and west, participating in the ancient ritual of the Twilight Barking as they called on the dogs of England to join in the search for the puppies.

Devoted fans of the book can continue their pursuit of the dalmatian trail beyond London and into Suffolk. Anne Grahame-Johnstone recalls that Dodie and Alec took her and her sister on a conducted tour of Suffolk, accompanied by Dandy the dalmatian. With the exception of Gainsborough's statue in Sudbury market place, Anne states that most of the locations outside London were made up of a mixture of various elements from Suffolk. However, don't go looking for the model for Hell Hall, as you won't find it. The lair of Cruella de Vil is the one entirely imaginary place in the story.

SWALLOWS AND AMAZONS

by *Arthur Ransome*

This classic children's adventure story of boats, pirates and buried treasure, has been a favourite ever since it was first published over 60 years ago. And as with many beloved children's books, the real story behind the writing of *Swallows and Amazons* is just as fascinating as the book itself. For instance, Arthur Ransome was married to a Russian who, in the months after the Russian Revolution, had been the personal secretary of the Communist statesman Trotsky. And years after *Swallows and Amazons* became a worldwide success, there was a battle between the people on whom the book's heroes were based, as bitter as any ever fought between the fictional characters.

★   ★   ★   ★   ★

THE STORY

The Walker children, John, Susan, Titty and Roger, are on holiday with their mother at Holly Howe, a farm on one of the shores of a lake in the Lake District. Their father, who is overseas with the Navy, sends a telegram granting his permission for them to go sailing, and the children spend their holiday as the crew of a dinghy called Swallow. Hard-headed John is Master; caring Susan is Mate; imaginative Titty is Able-Seaman and young Roger is Ship's Boy. Their mother allows them to camp on an island in the lake, but a crew from another small sailing craft, the Amazon, think that the island is rightfully theirs.

In the boat were two girls, one steering, the other sitting on the middle thwart. The two were almost exactly alike. Both had red knitted caps, brown shirts, blue knickerbockers, and no stockings. They were steering straight for the island.

The Swallows and the Amazons (the Blackett sisters, Nancy and Peggy) begin a friendly rivalry, but come together against a common enemy, Captain Flint (the Blackett's Uncle Jim). He is living on a houseboat on the lake, where he detests being disturbed as he is trying to write a book.

Houseboat Bay opened up. There was the houseboat and on the foredeck of her stood the fat man. 'He's very angry about something,' said Titty. He seemed to be shaking his fist at them, but they could not be sure, and presently they had passed the farther point and could not see him.

When Captain Flint's manuscript is stolen, he mistakenly thinks that John has had something to do with it. He is tipped the Black Spot by Nancy for doubting John's honesty, and in return, tries his best to put things right by arranging an exciting sea battle in Houseboat Bay. Captain Flint is made to walk the plank while begging for mercy, his crimes are wiped clean and the battle ends in a banquet.

On the last day of the children's holiday they go treasure-hunting on Cormorant Island, where Titty and Roger find Captain Flint's manuscript. It is inside his old sea chest which has been hidden there by thieves, and Captain Flint is overjoyed to have it returned to him.

The next day the children sadly leave the Lake District, but they are already looking forward to next year's holiday.

There were shouts of 'Goodbye', 'Remember the alliance', and 'Come again next year'. 'Three cheers for Wild Cat Island,' shouted John. They all cheered. 'Three cheers for the Swallows,' shouted Nancy. 'And for the Amazons,' they shouted back.

★　　★　　★　　★　　★

ARTHUR RANSOME

Arthur Mitchell Ransome was born in Leeds in 1884, the eldest of four children. As a boy, he showed marks of genius. For instance, by the age of four, he claimed to have read *Robinson Crusoe* from cover to cover. He also devised various schemes for making a fortune!

Every year, the Ransome family spent the summer holidays at Swainson's Farm in High Nibthwaite, at the south end of Coniston Water. The world around and on Coniston absorbed Arthur's life. He later recalled the time spent on Peel Island (the model for Wild Cat Island in *Swallows and Amazons*) as a time of summer bliss, spent running round the island like a savage.

It was after an unhappy first swimming lesson that Arthur taught himself to swim in only three visits to the public baths. His father had dropped Arthur into Coniston Water from a rowing boat, to see if he could swim spontaneously. Unfortunately, young Arthur's near-drowning experience meant he would never learn to swim in the usual way, and certainly not in Coniston Water.

In 1896, when Arthur was 12, the Ransomes encountered the Collingwood family picnicking on Peel Island. W G Collingwood was an artist and famous Lakeland writer who had come to Coniston to work with John Ruskin. It was the Collingwood children, Robin, Dora and Barbara, who taught Ransome to sail in their dinghy, Swallow.

In 1909 Ransome married Ivy Walker, with whom he had a daughter, Tabitha. However, the marriage was not a happy one, and in 1913, nurturing his ambitions of being a writer, he went to Russia. He saw the historic events of the Revolution at first hand, also coming to know Lenin, Trotsky and other leaders. In 1924 he married Evgenia Shelepin, who had been Trotsky's secretary. Ransome stayed in Russia as a foreign correspondent when the First World War broke out. (He was unfit to join the Army because of poor eyesight and ill health.) He continued his work as a journalist until 1929, when he was asked by *The Manchester Guardian* to go to Berlin as its correspondent.

Still troubled by his ill health, Ransome decided to abandon journalism and to concentrate on writing the children's story that he had been considering for several years. Direct inspiration for this came from the children of his old friend, Dora Collingwood, and her husband, Ernest Altounyan. Though they lived in Syria they returned every five years to Lanehead, near Coniston, to see Dora's parents. On a visit in 1928, Ernest bought a dinghy called Mavis for the children, while Ransome (who had become their honorary 'Uncle Arthur') bought them another called Swallow. In order to repay a birthday present of slippers given to him by the Altounyan children, Ransome decided to write them a story about Swallow, which rapidly grew into the tale of *Swallows and Amazons* as we know it today. It was dedicated 'To the six for whom it was written in exchange for a pair of slippers', though Ransome came in later years to regret this. He began to feel that the Altounyan family – Ernest in particular – were claiming some degree of credit for the books, and he decided to suppress the original dedication.

On its initial publication in July 1930, *Swallows and Amazons* received very favourable reviews but did not sell particularly well. However, within six years it was being acclaimed as a children's classic. A sequel,

Swallowdale, quickly followed, with Ransome eventually adding another ten books in the series.

★　　★　　★　　★　　★

THE TOUR

Start at The Museum of Lakeland Life in Kendal. This has a room devoted to Arthur Ransome which contains personal items such as manuscripts, drawings, photographs, letters and books. You can see the desk at which Arthur Ransome sat with his typewriter, his lucky holed stone from Coniston Old Man, and also his fishing rods, chess set and (as you might expect from reading *Swallows and Amazons*) a Jolly Roger flag.

Next head for the small town of Coniston itself, at the top end of Coniston Water. A mile to the east of Coniston, near the lakeside, is the Collingwood's family home, Lanehead. This was probably the model for Beckfoot, the home of the Amazons, and is now appropriately an outdoor pursuits centre. Next door is the model for Holly Howe, the home of the Swallows. Bank Ground Farm was the Altounyans' holiday home, though it is now a traditional Lakeland farmhouse offering bed and breakfast. You may recognise the house, as it is prominently featured at the beginning of the *Swallows and Amazons* film.

Continue down the road that follows the lake, passing first Peel Island on the right, and then Ransome's

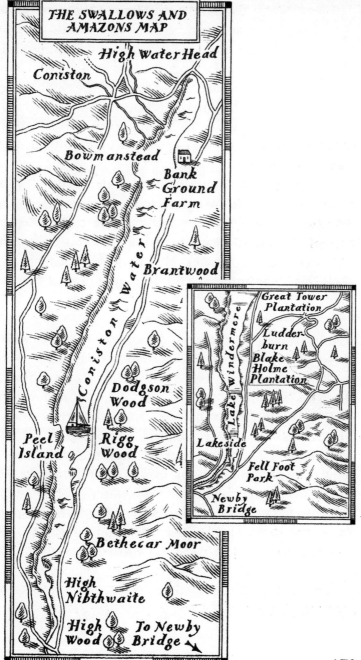

THE SWALLOWS AND AMAZONS MAP

High Water Head

Coniston

Bowmanstead

Bank Ground Farm

Brantwood

Coniston Water

Dodgson Wood

Peel Island

Rigg Wood

Bethecar Moor

High Nibthwaite

High Wood

To Newby Bridge

Great Tower Plantation

Lake Windermere

Ludderburn

Blake Holme Plantation

Lakeside

Fell Foot Park

Newby Bridge

childhood holiday home at High Nibthwaite. On reaching the main road, turn left towards Newby Bridge, and then towards Bowness-on-Windermere. Shortly after Blake Holme, turn right up past Great Tower Plantation. The second turn on the right brings you to Low Ludderburn, the house to which Arthur and Evgenia moved in 1925 and spent some of their happiest years.

The Ransomes finally left Low Ludderburn in 1940, during the Second World War as Evgenia wanted a place that had electricity and running water. Arthur bought the Heald, with land that fronted Coniston. He later lived at Lowick Hall in Lowick Green and made his final home at Hill Top cottage near Newby Bridge.

Arthur Ransome died on 3 June 1967 at Cheadle Royal Hospital near Manchester. His ashes were buried, according to his wishes, at St Paul's Church, Rusland, a couple of miles east of Low Ludderburn, lying between Coniston Water and Lake Windermere. The visitors' book in the church shows that Ransome has not been forgotten, as many readers have recorded their appreciation. 'Thank you Arthur Ransome for the stories of my childhood,' says one visitor. Another traveller from New Zealand writes, 'Arthur Ransome has given us much pleasure.' Another comment says simply, 'Swallows and Amazons forever!'

ANNE OF GREEN GABLES
by L M Montgomery

The adventures of the red-headed Anne Shirley take place at the end of the 19th century in the village of Avonlea on Prince Edward Island, off the coast of Eastern Canada. Beginning with her adoption as a loquacious 11-year-old by Marilla and Matthew Cuthbert, an elderly brother and sister, we follow the story of Anne's personal disappointments and social embarrassments to glorious success and academic achievement at college.

Though there is no Avonlea on Prince Edward Island, you do not have to look too hard at the author's life to discover that the novel is more or less a reworking of her own childhood. Lucy Maud Montgomery insisted on being called Maud and on spelling it without an 'e', just as Anne Shirley was furious at anyone careless enough to omit the 'e' from her Christian name. And in 1908, when *Anne of Green Gables* was published, Maud was living in her grandparents' farmhouse in the small village of Cavendish, 25 miles from the capital of Prince Edward Island, Charlottetown. The *Anne of Green Gables* trail therefore has a double attraction. Visitors can not only see the homes and villages where Maud Montgomery lived, but can also enjoy working out where fact ends and fiction begins; the two strands are intriguingly intertwined.

THE STORY

Anne Shirley is a skinny, red-haired orphan who erupts into the lives of an elderly brother and sister, Marilla and Matthew Cuthbert. To begin with her future looks bleak, as the Cuthberts had 'ordered' a boy, to be of help with the farm work. However, Matthew's heart melts when he picks Anne up at the station. He cannot tell her that there has been a mistake, and even the tough Marilla grudgingly agrees to keep her.

'Did you ever suppose you'd see the day when you'd be adopting an orphan girl? . . . goodness only knows what will come of it.'

The Cuthberts are soon charmed by the talkative child with the huge imagination. But fiery Anne has to learn to guard her tongue and control her temper, especially with Matthew and Marilla's friends and neighbours. Unfortunately she doesn't find self-control easy when people dare to mention the colour of her hair.

'I hate you,' she cried in a choked voice, stamping her foot on the floor. 'I hate you – I hate you – I hate you' a louder stamp with each assertion of hatred. 'How dare you call me skinny and ugly? How dare you say I'm freckled and red-headed? You are a rude, impolite, unfeeling woman!'

Anne causes many ups and downs at Green Gables and in the village. For example, Anne's dream of entertaining her best friend, Diana Barry, to tea ends in a nightmare when she mistakenly gives Diana currant wine instead of raspberry cordial to drink. Diana has three glassfuls, gets drunk and goes home in a terrible condition. Shortly afterwards, however, Anne is forgiven. She comes to the rescue when Diana's sister, Minnie May, gets croup. Anne single-handedly saves the child's life and Mrs Barry is forever in her debt.

People are alternately exasperated and entertained by Anne, but as she grows up she brings happiness and love to all she meets. Everyone is delighted when she wins a scholarship to college. However, Matthew sadly dies, and Anne decides to give up the scholarship in order to work as a teacher, look after Marilla, and prevent the sale of Green Gables.

> *. . . but if the path set before her feet was to be narrow she knew that flowers of quiet happiness would bloom along it. The joys of sincere work and worthy aspiration and congenial friendship were to be hers; nothing could rob her of her birthright of fancy or her ideal world of dreams. And there was always the bend in the road!*

★　★　★　★　★

L M MONTGOMERY

Lucy Maud Montgomery was born on 30 November 1874 in New London, Canada. She lived at a house called Clifton Corner until her mother died in 1876, when Maud was two years old. Her father moved away to the west of Canada and, like Anne Shirley, Maud was sent to live with an elderly couple: Alexander and Lucy MacNeill, her maternal grandparents. Also like Anne, Maud's ambitions were thwarted when her grandfather died in 1898, leaving her at the age of 23 to look after her grandmother. But living in her grandparents' farmhouse provided the inspiration for Green Gables.

Maud became a prolific writer of poems and short stories and eventually embarked on a novel. But when five publishers rejected *Anne of Green Gables*, she threw the manuscript into a hat box and abandoned it. When she happened to come across it 18 months later, she tried one more time and sent it to a new publisher in Boston. The book was immediately accepted and on publication became an instant bestseller, leading to a series of five sequels. Unhappily, protracted litigation with the publisher left Maud Montgomery with just a small fraction of her rightful royalties on the book.

At the age of 37, after the death of her grandmother, Maud was married to the Reverend Ewen Macdonald. In her journals, Maud records how she wept the night before her wedding at the realisation that she was not marrying for romance but more for convenience. She left Prince Edward Island, never to live there again, though all her novels continued to be set there. Maud had two sons, but never seemed to have found the contentment that Anne Shirley finds in her stories. Maud was highly-strung, suffering depressions and nervous breakdowns throughout her life. In many ways, Anne Shirley is the outgoing, happy-go-lucky girl that Maud longed to be.

Maud died at the age of 67, asking to be buried in the cemetery at Cavendish, next to the Haunted Woods and almost in sight of Green Gables.

THE TOUR

Prince Edward Island is Canada's smallest province, being 140 miles long and 40 miles wide, with a population of 130,000 (no more than an English town the size of Swindon). The island lies off the coast of New Brunswick and Nova Scotia, a 30-minute plane ride from Halifax.

Hunter River is the model for Bright River, to which Matthew travels in the buggy with the sorrel mare to collect Anne. Sadly, the railway station where they first met has now been demolished. A 20-minute drive north from Hunter River is the first stop on the tour: the Lucy Maud Montgomery Birthplace Museum at Clifton Corner, New London.

Next, continue on to 'Avonlea' itself – in fact, the town of Cavendish. Anne describes Prince Edward Island as 'the bloomiest place', and the countryside around Cavendish is delightful. The fields are neat and well kept; sometimes lush grass grazed by small herds of cows, sometimes large rectangular patches of deep red earth where the potatoes are grown. The

179

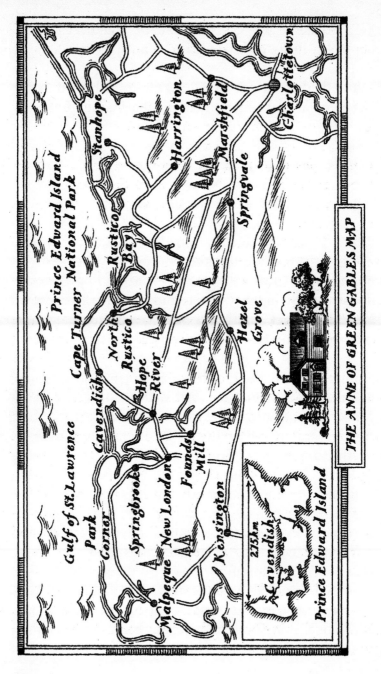

THE ANNE OF GREEN GABLES MAP

farmhouses are usually smart white-timbered buildings, nearly always with a bulky Dutch barn to one side.

Follow the signs to the site of Maud Montgomery's home. The farmhouse where Maud grew up with her grandparents, and where she wrote *Anne of Green Gables*, has unfortunately been pulled down. But the property is still in the possession of the family. Jennie MacNeill, wife of a great-grandson of Maud's grandparents, runs a small museum on the site.

If it was Maud's grandparents' home that provided the general inspiration for the book, it was Green Gables – a nearby house owned by another set of relatives – which offered the exact setting. It's here that you will find the Lover's Lane and Haunted Woods of the novel. The house itself was bought by the federal government in 1936 and placed under the control of the Prince Edward Island National Park. It was restored and furnished to portray the period setting as described in the novel, so outside and inside it looks every inch the Green Gables of the book. A leaflet available from the house has a map showing the path around Cavendish which takes you to the main Montgomery sights, though the sense of place is so exact that you could almost find your way around with just a copy of *Anne of Green Gables*.

For the best of the Montgomery museums, go to Park Corner. The time that Maud spent as a child at this house with her Campbell cousins seems to have been among the happiest days of her life. You will recognise the pond before the house as the Lake of Shining Waters of the novel. Park Corner is still in the same family, and is now owned by George Campbell, who gave up farming to concentrate on developing the museum. It was at Park Corner that Maud was married, and today, as *Anne of Green Gables* is hugely popular in Japan, many Japanese couples come to the house to do the same.

THE LITTLE PRINCE
by Antoine de Saint-Exupéry

If you visit France, check your change and one very striking banknote will almost certainly catch your eye. The 50-franc note shows the portrait of a balding man next to a slice of the world map. At the top soars an old single-wing aircraft. At the bottom stands the drawing of a young boy with a shock of yellow hair wearing a blue bow-tie and white bell-bottom trousers. In the top left-hand corner stands something that looks like a hat but which, on closer study, turns out to be a small elephant inside the belly of a snake.

The Little Prince,
illustrated by Antoine de Saint-Exupéry.

This extraordinary banknote shows images from one of France's most famous books, *The Little Prince*, together with its author, Antoine de Saint-Exupéry. Intended as a story for children, *The Little Prince* has become hugely popular among adult readers, who enjoy its unique mixture of fantasy, poetry, practical science, curious imaginings and simple happiness.

If you wanted to visit a place that matched the exact setting of *The Little Prince*, you would have to mount a camel and head into the arid wastes of the Sahara Desert. Fortunately, this won't be necessary, as you can visit a place in south-west France which was far more crucial to the writing of the book.

THE STORY

The narrator is flying an aeroplane over Africa's Sahara Desert when he has to make a crash landing on the sand. To his surprise he quickly discovers he is not alone – he has a companion: a little prince. This small, golden-haired visitor appears at dawn and asks the crashed pilot for a drawing of a sheep. The pilot eventually learns the little prince's story. His new companion is a traveller from Asteroid B-612, which is so small that it is in constant danger of being over-run by baobab trees.

> . . . *the planet the little prince came from was scarcely any larger than a house!*

184

The little prince's life consists of keeping the baobabs under control, cleaning out his two active and one extinct volcanoes, and watching the sunsets. (The smallness of his asteroid means that he could watch a sunset 44 times a day if he chooses.) He also takes great care in tending a rose, his pride and joy.

> *. . . the little prince could not restrain his admiration: 'Oh! How beautiful you are!' 'Am I not?' the flower responded, sweetly. 'And I was born at the same moment as the sun . . .'*

One morning, the little prince decides to visit the neighbouring asteroids in order to look for knowledge. He first meets a vain king who thinks he can control the stars. Next he encounters a conceited man who longs to be admired. A drunkard lives on the third asteroid, who drinks to forget that he is ashamed... of drinking. On the fourth planet is a businessman, who counts the stars in the belief that he owns them.

> *'And what good does it do you to own the stars?' 'It does me the good of making me rich.' 'And what good does it do you to be rich?' 'It makes it possible for me to buy more stars, if any are discovered.'*

On the fifth planet, he meets a lamplighter who spends his life obeying orders. The sixth planet is home to a geographer, who directs him to the seventh planet: Earth.

When he lands, the little prince is very surprised not

to see any people and thinks that he has perhaps come to the wrong planet. He meets a snake who explains that he is in the desert, where there are no people. The lonely little prince then sets off to look for company and comes across a fox, who teaches him how to love. The fox tells him his 'very simple secret':

It is only with the heart that one can see rightly; what is essential is invisible to the eye.

The little prince sadly leaves the fox and continues on his quest for knowledge. Each person he meets on Earth leaves him yearning to be back on his asteroid, controlling his baobab trees, cleaning out his volcanoes, and tending to his rose.

Finally the little prince meets up with the narrator, and they set off across the desert to look for water. Eventually finding a well, they are both refreshed and the narrator manages to fix his plane. Sadly, the little prince decides that he also must return home to the stars.

ANTOINE DE SAINT-EXUPÉRY

Antoine de Saint-Exupéry was born in France's second largest city, Lyon, on 29 June 1900. He was just three years old when the Wright Brothers made the first powered flight in North Carolina on 17 December 1903, but this event determined Saint-Exupéry's future just as it changed the history of the world. As a young man, he developed a passion for aeroplanes, and, after leaving the University of Fribourg, he joined the French air force in 1921.

In 1926, Saint-Exupéry became a pilot with the Aeropostale service, newly set up in Toulouse. With flying still very much in its infancy, carrying the air mail was a dangerous business. There were huge risks in flying over big mountains with only primitive radios and inadequate navigational instruments. Saint-Exupéry loved flying and enjoyed taking chances. But it was after he left the air mail service, in 1935, that he almost killed himself when he crashed into the North African desert. Like the aviator in *The Little Prince,* while he and his passenger survived the crash, they almost died of thirst.

During the Second World War, when France was invaded by the Germans, Saint-Exupéry took refuge in New York, awaiting the time when he could help join the fight to liberate his homeland. He used his experience of flying to write a series of books which became classics: *Southern Mail, Night Flight,* and *Wind, Sand and Stars. The Little Prince,* his best-known book, was suggested to him by his American publisher who at lunch one day watched Saint-Exupéry doodling the outline of a small figure. The publisher suggested that the little fellow in the drawing should be turned into a children's story.

Shortly after finishing *The Little Prince*, Saint-Exupéry returned to Europe and joined the Free French forces. On 31 July 1944, while flying a reconnaissance mission over occupied France, his aircraft disappeared without trace over the sea. He was aged 44.

THE TOUR

Situated in the bottom left-hand corner of the country, Toulouse is France's fourth biggest city, though it has more the feel of a small lively country town. The city centre, which spreads out from the huge Place du Capitole, is where you should head first. It has changed very little since Saint-Exupéry first arrived here in the autumn of 1926, when after some false starts to his career, and with frustrated hopes of becoming a writer, he was determined to make a success of his newly-found job as air mail pilot.

With the others who worked for the Latecoere company, Saint-Exupéry was put up at the Hotel du Grand Balcon at 8 Rue Romiguieres, which can be found at the north-western corner of the Place du Capitole. The owner of the hotel, Monsieur Jean Brousse, has manned the reception here for over 41 years, and the hallway of the hotel is decorated with memorabilia. The posters and photographs of the old air mail pilots – all every inch dashing young men in their flying machines – of course include Saint-Exupéry. The real place of pilgrimage for *Little Prince* fans is Saint-Exupéry's room: Room 32. Seen from the outside, the room sits just above the 'Hotel' sign. Inside it has been faithfully maintained just as it was when Saint-Exupéry slept in it.

The five years that Saint-Exupéry spent as a mail pilot seem to have been the happiest and most productive of his life: he gained all the inspiration for his books while working as a professional aviator. Life for a flier was tough. An old Ford bus would pull up outside the Hotel to take the pilots to the airfield at Montaudran at four o'clock in the morning. (Anyone who missed the bus was in very serious trouble!)

Much of Saint-Exupéry's off-duty time in Toulouse was spent in the Café-Restaurant Lafayette in Place Wilson, a five minute walk away. Place Wilson is still there – a handsome oval of solid brick-built shops and restaurants with an attractive small park area in the centre. The Bistro Romain was formerly the Café-Restaurant Lafayette itself. As you sit at a pavement table, it is easy to imagine Saint-Exupéry sitting here 70 years previously, his head buried in a favourite book, scribbling notes for his stories, maybe sketching some rudimentary drawings for the tiny character who would one day become the little prince.

While in Toulouse you should spare time to see what

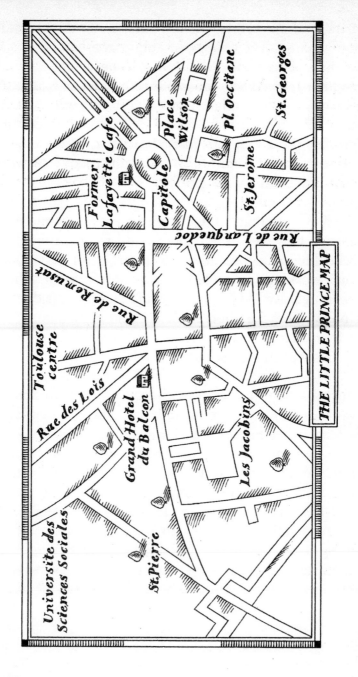

THE LITTLE PRINCE MAP

St. Georges

Pl. Occitane

St. Jerome

Place Wilson

Capitole

Former Lafayette Cafe

Rue de Languedoc

Rue de Remusat

Toulouse centre

Rue des Lois

Grand Hotel du Balcon

Les Jacobins

Universite des Sciences Sociales

St. Pierre

190

happened to the small scale aviation business that Saint-Exupéry helped to develop. Aerospatiale is one of Europe's major aircraft builders. At its plant on Avenue Jean Monnet at Colomiers you can visit the assembly line of the Airbus A340 and 330 planes. In the Sixties, it was here that Concorde made its maiden voyage, little more than 25 years after Saint-Exupéry made his last fatal flight. Just imagine what he – and the little prince – would have made of supersonic travel!

Bibliography

The following books have been an invaluable source of reference:

Alice's Adventures in Wonderland
Hudson, Derek, *Lewis Carroll*, Constable, 1954.

Carrie's War
Bawden, Nina, *In My Own Time*, Little, Brown & Co, 1995.

Christmas Carol, A
Ackroyd, Peter, *Dickens*, Sinclair-Stevenson, 1990.

Danny, The Champion of the World
Treglown, Jeremy, *Roald Dahl*, Faber & Faber, 1995.

Hundred and One Dalmatians, The
Grove, Valerie, *Dear Dodie: The Life of Dodie Smith*,
Chatto & Windus, 1996.

Little Prince, The
Webster, Paul, *Antoine de Saint-Exupéry: The Life and Death of the
Little Prince*, Macmillan, 1994

Lorna Doone
Dunn, Waldo Hilary, *R.D. Blackmore*, Hale, 1956.

Peter Pan
Birkin, Andrew, *J. M. Barrie and the Lost Boys*, Constable, 1979.

Railway Children, The
Briggs, Julia, *A Woman of Passion: The Life of E. Nesbit*, Century
Hutchison, 1987.

Secret Garden, The
Thwaite, Ann, *Waiting for the Party*, Faber & Faber, 1994.

Swallows and Amazons
Brogan, Hugh, *The Life of Arthur Ransome*, Cape, 1984.
Hardyment, Christina, *Arthur Ransome and Captain Flint's Trunk*,
Cape, 1984.

Thomas the Tank Engine
Sibley, Brian, *The Thomas the Tank Engine Man*, Heinemann, 1995.

Watership Down
Adams, Richard, *The Day Gone By*, Penguin, 1991.

Wind in the Willows, The
Green, Peter, *Beyond the Wild Wood, the World of Kenneth Grahame*, Webb & Bower, 1982.

Winnie-the-Pooh
Milne, Christopher, *The Enchanted Place*, Minerva, 1994.
Thwaite, Ann, *A A Milne: His Life*, Faber, 1990.
Thwaite, Ann, *The Brilliant Career of Winnie-the-Pooh*, Methuen, 1992.

General
Carpenter, Humphrey, *Secret Gardens*, Allen & Unwin, 1985.
Carpenter, Humphrey and Pritchard, Mari, *The Oxford Companion to Children's Literature*, Oxford, 1984.
Lurie, Alison, *Don't Tell the Grown-Ups*, Bloomsbury, 1990.
Wullschlager, Jackie, *Inventing Wonderland*, Methuen, 1995.

Index

This index contains the key authors, books and map locations.